Dark Music

Janis Susan May

*To Arvona —
Happy Reading!
Janis Susan May*

Vintage Romance Publishing

Goose Creek, South Carolina

www.vrpublishing.com

Janis Susan May

Dark Music

ISBN: *0-9785368-0-0*

PUBLISHED BY VINTAGE ROMANCE PUBLISHING, LLC

www.vrpublishing.com

Dedication

*To Marilyn Mathis Spaulding and John
Spaulding, beloved and extraordinary
friends*

And

*Hiram M. Patterson,
The most wonderful man in the world!*

Chapter One

The wheels were spinning out of control again. I eased the car down into second gear and let it slide sickeningly across the ice until the tires caught on a patch of dry pavement. This time the car slid almost to the snow bank before the tires finally took hold and sent the car forward again.

I heaved a sigh of relief and cursed the name, head and lineage of the car rental agent in Banff who had told me the road was clear all the way to Mountain Lake Spa. Maybe he called this snow-lined, ice-patched corkscrew strip of paving clear, but I, a resident of sun-blest New Orleans, found it anything else but. If I hadn't lived a year in New York, I probably would have turned tail and come in with Bernie, Anita and the rest of them in the chartered plane.

If I had weakened and let Kevin come along, he would have loved it; the private plane, the press conference...

No. The thought of Kevin confined in the same plane with Vanessa and Clement was mind-boggling. We would have to have driven.

And if we had, Kevin would have insisted on an automatic shift. He found my insistence on manual cars amusing, dismissing my dislike of automatic transmissions as a dip into the ever-expanding pool of this new women's lib, a childish whim he would eventually help me overcome.

He thought!

I shifted up into third again, taking advantage of a rare straight shot of road. The others must have gotten there hours ago, but not for anything would I have confined myself in a small plane with them, no matter how exotic the experience. It would be bad enough to spend four days with them at the conference.

The conference. This was the first conference just for romance writers and readers that I had ever heard of. A new and burgeoning field, romance publishing had taken the world by storm, earning the disdain of the women's libbers, the adoration of women readers all over the country and the delight of publishers, whose business was steadily dwindling in this new era of television.

I didn't belong at a romance writers' conference any more than I deserved to be included in Wingate Publications' top romantic lineup, whimsically dubbed 'The Fabulous Four' by some reporter when we had all, somewhat freakishly, been on some best-seller list the same week. I had only written two books, and only one of them had been a romance, but Bernie had been insistent that I attend.

"I need you there, Liz," he had repeated, as usual, using the name he himself had given me. Such was the power of Bernard Wingate that now nearly everyone called me Liz Allison. My real name of Elizabeth MacAllister would probably have been forgotten had it not been used on *A Woman of Quality*, my first, decidedly non-romance, novel.

And my other name, the one I had carried for such a short time...I tried not to think about that one at all.

"I'm afraid he's quite set on it, Elizabeth," his wife Anita had added. She had championed my first book, which had repaid her by becoming a critical success, and she wept when Bernie had cajoled me into writing a vividly suggestive and wholly unbelievable romantic fantasy of the kind critics called bodice-rippers. He titled it *Sisters of Desire*, and it had repaid him by becoming one of his highest grossing books ever.

"But I don't want to go to Canada," I had said.

It was true; I hadn't, and I still didn't, and yet, here I was, grimly fighting my way up an icy road beneath a lowering gray sky. Why was I always being put in situations I didn't want to be in? Kevin would be expecting an answer when I got home, and I didn't have the foggiest idea of what to tell him.

"Would I ask you to go all that way if I didn't need you?" Bernie had put on the sad-beagle expression that he had almost patented.

"Of course you would, just the way you asked me to go all the way to New York for a story conference on *Daughters* that could just as easily have been done by phone," I had answered with more truth than tact. "You just want Wingate Publications to make a big showing."

He had been entirely unabashed. "Can't afford not to. We need our 'Fabulous Four' to be there. The publicity..."

"You're starting to believe your own press, Bernard," Anita had said with an indulgent laugh. "Tell me, Elizabeth, have you done much on *A Man of Honor*?"

It had been a ticklish situation; both books were intended as sequels to my previous novels, and each of the Wingates thought I should work exclusively on the one they favored.

"Of course not. She's working on *Daughters*." Bernie had beamed with anticipation, his voice only slightly tinged with the unmistakable edge of an order. "And she's going to have it finished by the conference, aren't you?"

Well, I hadn't. Not only was *Daughters of Passion* not finished, it wasn't much further along than when I had talked to the Wingates. Neither was *A Man of Honor*. Both Bernie and Anita would be furious with me.

That was only fair; I was not too happy with them, either. I still wasn't quite sure how they had done it, but even knowing my dislike of public speaking they had enrolled me as a lecturer at the 'Just Write for Love Conference', on the subject of 'Creating Quality Romantic Fiction', no less. Bernie had told me only after the programs had been printed, so I really couldn't drop out, but I had refused categorically to ride in the chartered plane with Jane and Clement and Vanessa. I didn't particularly like any of them, and knowing Bernie, there would be a full-blown media circus waiting when they landed.

An ice patch threw the car sideways; I hadn't been vigilant enough, and it took some wild wheel-turning to bring it under control again. Another thing I hadn't bargained for was snow over my head in the middle of April. I was freezing despite the snug warmth of my old fur jacket and the best effort of the car's heater. I'd probably stay cold until I got home.

Once, a couple of lifetimes ago, someone had teased

me about having thin Rebel blood. At least, it had been teasing before that and everything else between us turned ugly.

The road did two more nasty turns and then dipped down into the wide parking lot of the hotel. Like something from another century and another continent, the elegant Mountain Lake Spa rose high and proud over the still-frozen lake, but by that time I was so tired and tense I really didn't care. I was here to deliver a talk, and I would do it to the best of my ability; however, I had not promised to enjoy it. Little did I know that the time would come when doing nothing more than just giving a silly speech sounded like the most desirable thing in the world.

* * *

Despite my fatigue and general grumpiness, the lobby of the Mountain Lake Spa was breathtaking. I stood still for a moment, allowing the formal beauty and order to spread over me like a healing balm. Maybe I should have let Kevin come along. He admired antiques and the trappings of gracious living. Maybe in this romantic setting I could...

Good grief! I was starting to think rubbish as bad as I was writing. Deciding whether or not to marry Kevin should be done with rationality and cool logic, not in a fog of artificial romance. I knew that didn't work. But...Kevin would love it here.

Built in a gentler age, when space was admired for its own merit, the lobby soared upward to the second story on a row of enormous marble columns. The far wall was a series of high arched windows framing the most incredible view of tall mountains coming down into a tiny bowl in which lay a perfect frozen jewel of a lake.

Later, I would notice the oak chairs, tables and the overstuffed couches that filled the lobby, the row of enticing shops, the comfortable bar behind the short, freestanding walls, but now all I could see was that incredible expanse of snow, ice and mountains before me. Just outside the window was a broad esplanade that must be heaven in the summertime. Beyond that was a blank expanse of snow that must cover grass. The lake was fringed with large rocks, their frosty grayness the only definition between snow-covered ground and snow-covered ice. A skating rink had been scraped off and defined by a border of smaller stones. Far out in the middle of the lake a lopsided snowman sat in solitary splendor.

I gasped, all resolutions not to succumb to the beauties of this place forgotten. What a place to set a novel. How could anyone ignore the antique charm of the hotel, the glory of the natural setting, the encroaching and shadowy woods...?

Perhaps a period piece? Not the frontier; that was overdone and really not glamorous enough for this ambiance. The First World War? Maybe. It was a time in history not yet littered with historical romances, and a time of high emotions; the only drawback was that the clothes then were so ugly...

"Ah, another starry-eyed mountain watcher!"

I recognized that theatrical drawl and gritted my teeth. Don't get me wrong, I have nothing against those whose preferences differed from the norm, but Clement

Wallingford would have been an obnoxious human being no matter what he chose to sleep with.

Well over six feet tall and lanky, he wore his black-dyed hair shoulder length and affected loosely tied silk scarves in place of ties. One of the biggest moneymakers in Bernie's stable, Clement's name never appeared on any book cover; instead he hid behind Aurora Wall (who wrote nauseatingly sweet love stores simply dripping with sticky sentiment) and Jessica Fordham (whose ultra-sexy books had occasionally been classed with pornography). Both sold very well, and until the true authorship had been disclosed in a singularly nasty tabloid *exposé*, reviewers occasionally complimented their true understanding of a woman's innermost feelings.

"Liz, dear girl, how wonderful to see you..." He squealed in a low roar that didn't quite reach the second floor.

I never knew if Clement made a conscious effort to impersonate a 1940s stereotype of a siren or not, but his walk was pure Joan Crawford. His long-fingered hands, always cold and powdery-dry, closed around mine in limp salute.

"Hello, Clement. I didn't know if you would be here yet or not." I retrieved my hands as quickly as was decent.

He gestured expressively. "We've been here for hours and hours...Dear Bernie was more than a teeny bit annoyed that you weren't with us for the press conference, but now he can relax because 'The Fabulous Four' is complete, and all of his top scribes are safely under his wing at last."

I followed his sweeping gesture with ill-concealed resignation. I had met most of Bernie's authors, including the other members of the so-called 'Fabulous Four' and didn't care much for any of them. The other two members of the 'Four' were ensconced in the bar and looked like they had been there for some time.

Vanessa Mangold and Jane Hall were just about as different as two people could be. Vanessa (neé Sophie Goldberg) favored big-brimmed hats and floral prints. She wrote four sure-fire best sellers a year and passionately believed all the cloyingly sentimental drivel she wrote about love being an overwhelming force which only happened once in a lifetime, a spiritual bond that transcended death.

I had believed that once, too.

More fool me.

Despite her prodigious output Vanessa all but lived on the lecture circuit, speaking to church groups and women's' clubs about the place of women in the scheme of things, extolling the virtues of home and husband. In my own cynical way I found that amusing, for not only had Vanessa never married, she was practically an industry in herself. While she preached the gospel of feminine subservience, she traveled around the world, ran several companies and made a fantastic amount of money, all without a man in sight.

She said she was waiting for Mr. Right. She looked like she had been waiting a long time.

Jane Hall was another kind of cat altogether. Small, mousy and pinch-faced, she looked more like a grocery store checker than a one-woman empire. She wrote under so many pseudonyms, it was a wonder if she could remember them all, churning out umpteen books a year in a variety of genres with assembly line precision. Rumor had it that she was thinking of branching off and forming her own publishing company. I didn't think there was much to it, but the idea had Bernie absolutely panicked. Jane Hall was his biggest moneymaker.

There were other people there, too. I saw Ralph Harcourt, an editor for one of our biggest competitors. I was sure that in the sparse crowd there were other editors, just as I was sure that somewhere in that bright-eyed gaggle of expectant faces there were a few professional writers beyond the one or two I recognized. The majority of conferees wouldn't arrive until tomorrow, since the conference didn't begin officially until the day after, but there were always a few hopefuls who came early, as if it would give them extra points.

"You will join us for a drink, won't you, Liz?"

"I've got to check in and find my room..."

"Nonsense." Clement trilled a musical little laugh designed for an Edwardian debutante. "It won't take a minute to register, and we've got so much to talk about..."

I couldn't think of a thing that Clement, Vanessa, Jane and I had to discuss, but I had also learned that it was easier to go along with whatever Clement proposed. The waspish ill humor that inevitably followed his being crossed was legendary.

"All right...just give me a minute."

"Welcome to the Mountain Lake Spa," said the pretty young woman behind the desk.

"Thank you. It's a beautiful place. All those mountains and those trees...I'm overwhelmed. I've lived in New Orleans all my life," I added in needless explanation. Talking too much had always been one of my great failings, as I had often been told.

It wasn't a complete lie. I had lived in New Orleans *almost* all my life; there was no need to bring up—even to myself—that year in New York, that wonderful, funny, miserable year I was working so hard and so futilely to block out of my memory.

"Not many mountains there," she agreed. "Do you have a reservation?"

"Yes. Elizabeth MacAllister."

The pretty young clerk flipped through the box of reservation cards, then, frowning slightly, dug through them again. "I'm sorry, Miss MacAllister, but I don't show anything..."

I had forgotten how Bernie's mind worked. "What about Liz Allison?"

Success. She smiled, picked out a card and handed over a registration form. "Here, Miss Allison. If you'd just fill this out...?"

How like Bernie to use the name he had invented for me. "I hope it faces the lake."

"Oh, yes, Miss Allison. Mr. Wingate specifically requested lakefront rooms."

"My name is MacAllister," I said, handing the card back to her. "Allison is only a pen name."

"Yes, Miss MacAllister," she said promptly. Apparently, she had gotten a crash course in the ways of writers. "Your room is on the second floor, in one of the towers. The view is lovely."

Tipping the bellboy, I sent him on up with the luggage, then joined the hovering Clement and headed for the bar. It would be easiest to get this enforced conviviality over with as soon as possible; hopefully, I could plead fatigue and get away fairly early. Writers are not the most social of creatures under the best of circumstances and especially not with other writers.

"And here she is...at last!" With a flourish Clement pulled out one of the overstuffed chairs for me.

"Liz." Vanessa nodded regally, hardly making her girlish curls bob at all. "How delightful to see you again, my dear."

Each word was enunciated with painful precision, which to those lucky ones who really knew her could only mean one thing; she was as drunk as the proverbial skunk.

"Hello," Jane said. She rarely said more than was absolutely necessary, apparently saving all her words for the printed page.

Sinking into the soft chair, I acknowledged their greetings with equal enthusiasm, then ordered a vodka tonic from the hovering waitress and sat back to survey the magnificent view. It was much more interesting than any of my companions.

The bar was built in a semi-circle, with three of those enormous arched windows facing the frozen lake. Little wooden half-walls the height of a tall man enclosed the area, blocking it off from the rest of the lobby. They looked new and strangely harsh, in contrast to the aged patina of the rest of the place. In the corner there was a pretty girl seated at a troubadour harp, and the throbbing plaint of an ancient Irish ballad threaded softly through the babble of conversation. Behind her was a shrouded piano.

I stared at it curiously. It had taken me a long time to be able to see a piano without a rush of emotion, and I wasn't really sure I had mastered the trick yet.

The waitress brought my drink and went on to deliver a tray full of nasty-looking pink concoctions to a table of giggling, middle-aged matrons. They all looked just too excited for words. It would be too much to hope that they were here with their husbands for an insurance meeting or something...

No, that would indeed be too much. Already they were looking overtly at our table, whispering to each other and pointing. Clement glared back at them with distaste and more than a little jealousy.

Sighing, he turned his attention back to us. "Bitches. It is amazing how dear Bernie could talk us all into attending this farce."

"Hardly a farce. These are fans. They buy our books, which makes us money."

"Not enough to socialize with them. I mean, just look at them..."

"There might even be some good writing talent here. There are more coming in tomorrow, remember?"

He sighed again, this time even more dramatically. "Really, Liz! You go beyond charity!"

"What I don't see..." Vanessa said slowly, adding the onion from her Gibson to the pile already on the table. It looked like a fair-sized crop. "...is why we should be expected to help people who might become our rivals?"

"Exactly!" Clement agreed quickly. "It's like cutting our own throats."

"Bullshit."

We all looked at Jane in surprise. It was so rare that she spoke without being spoken directly to first that it took a moment to realize who was talking.

"That is a singularly inelegant word." Clement's voice was dangerously silky.

"It's an inelegant subject. There's always enough business if your books are good enough. If they aren't, you shouldn't be writing."

"That's easy enough for you to say...You're practically taking over the industry all by yourself..."

Surprisingly, it was Vanessa who laid a slightly wobbly hand on Clement's arm. His normally papery-pale face had gone a dark red. "We don't need a scene, Clement. There are probably reporters here."

Since he had suffered at the hands of reporters before, the argument had a salutary restraining effect on Clement. He took a gulp of his drink and then smiled nastily.

"Well, my dears, have you started on your novel in this lovely setting yet?"

Vanessa shrugged. Her hat had listed about five degrees to the left and was struggling to hold the position. "It's so like other hotels of the period..."

"Jane?" he pressed. By now his skin had recovered its usual pallor. He looked as if he never exercised or came out in the daylight. More than once, unkind types had speculated on his being some sort of vampire.

"Really, Clement," she answered in her precise little voice.

Vanessa and Clement were excessive, obvious, but Jane Hall was something else. The few times we had met, I had learned exactly nothing about her; she questioned nothing, answered nothing and generally said nothing. Sometimes it was easy to forget that she was there. I wondered how she poured forth such a wealthy of lushly romantic writing when there didn't appear to have ever been any romance in her life. Dreaming? Wish fulfillment? Who knew? Anyway, my romantic life wasn't so great that I could throw stones. I had already had one spectacular, painful failure, and now there was Kevin...

"Mountain watching again, Liz? I asked you..."

"I heard you, Clement. We're none of us going to do a book set up here, and you know it. At least, not now." I grinned and nodded towards the other tables. "After this conference the market will be glutted with books about old hotels in the mountains by a lake."

He sighed, dramatically, of course. "Too true, too true. What a pity the amateurs get to have a crack at it. It would be too perfect..."

"For Aurora or Jessica?"

"Both, my dear, both! The woods, the natural beauty...Aurora could patter on for hours. And Jessica..." Clement leered, and then smoothed his eyebrow with a well-manicured fingertip.

"I should hope she'd wait for summer. She'd freeze otherwise."

It was a standard thing in every one of his Jessica

Fordham books to have at least one episode of *al fresco* lovemaking. Clement got it at once, tossing his head back and laughing loudly enough to attract the attention of all the other tables. Vanessa looked prettily blank for a short moment then permitted herself a small giggle while apostrophizing me as a naughty girl. Her hat listed another degree or two. Jane merely sat there, unsmiling, her flat nickel eyes unwinking.

"It has been a pleasure seeing all of you again," she said with cool and palpable untruth. "I'm sure we will have many chances to talk in the coming days. You will all be at the dinner tonight? Good afternoon." Clutching her purse, Jane Hall rose suddenly and swiftly walked away without a backward glance or waiting for any response from us.

At least Clement waited until she was at the elevators, across the lobby and safely out of earshot. "Damned peculiar woman."

Vanessa shuddered delicately. Her hat held on for dear life. "She gives me the horrors. There's something not quite...natural about her." Uttered while in Clement's presence, that was quite a condemnation indeed.

"She is unusual," I said, trying to be fair.

"If she is a woman," Clement said in a poisonously lewd voice.

I couldn't stand it any longer. Vanessa's missish posturings and Clement's nasty, sexist tongue were at least as offensive as Jane's supercilious hauteur. I thought that as far as they were concerned, Jane's major sin was in outselling them both. For a moment I toyed with the idea of telling them so then reconsidered. It probably wouldn't do any good, and if I were to scrape through this conference I didn't need them down on me — though they would probably turn on me as soon as my back was turned.

I picked up my purse and discarded coat. "Well, I'm going to go find my room and lie down."

"Alone? What a waste of time," Clement sniggered suggestively, and suddenly, I was reminded of a white, unhealthy looking slug, the nasty kind that lives under rotting logs and damp rocks. Clement had never been one of my favorite people, but now I found him positively revolting.

Vanessa's eyes flashed, and I realized that my thoughts had shown on my face. It is an old fault, and there's nothing I can do about it. I don't dare play poker. Kevin says my transparency of emotions is as good as a lie detector. He says he likes it.

He would.

"Your face is like glass," he had said once, not realizing that in doing so he echoed another, deeper, more beloved voice which had said the same thing sometime long ago on a happy afternoon. There had been a lush carpet of grass and a big shady tree and champagne out of paper cups...

"Lith, dearrr," Vanessa's voice pierced my memories. Her enunciation was slipping as fast as her hat. "Are you all right? You look so..."

I nodded at her so abruptly it sent my head spinning. "I'm just tired. It was a long drive."

Suddenly, it seemed not only a long drive, but a long life. How could I have hoped that a few days respite would change the situation? Kevin was waiting for an answer to his proposal, and while I was unsure about marrying him, I was loath to lose him. In the fear of doing the wrong thing, I had taken refuge in doing nothing.

I didn't know what to do.

I couldn't afford another mistake.

Chapter Two

A bath made me feel better. I soaked in the big tub then toweled dry with one of the enormous peach colored bath sheets.

There wasn't much time to luxuriate. Bernie was expecting all of us to meet him for cocktails that night, and then there would be a Wingate Publications meeting tomorrow, which was why we had all been summoned a day early. Trust Bernie to work in a meeting with his own writers at minimal cost to himself.

The bathroom was fairly warm. My shiver was purely that of anticipation. Bernie was already upset with me, and it could only get worse. My new book was late, and he had no patience with that.

The telephone rang. I delayed answering it long enough to slip into my heavy robe. The bedroom radiators were going full tilt, but it still felt cold to me.

"Elizabeth?"

There was no need wondering who it was. Even if the determinedly cultured voice hadn't given her away, she was the only person here who ever called me Elizabeth. That name belonged to my old lifetime.

"Hello, Anita."

Bernie Wingate's wife was the exact opposite of her husband. Tall, willowy and studiedly beautiful, she looked almost a generation younger than her actual age, an illusion she worked hard to maintain, just as she worked hard to maintain her socialite status. She succeeded at both, for to look at her no one would ever have guessed that she was rising fifty, or that she had been born and brought up in one of New York's worst slums, which was just what she intended.

I had discovered the secret of her origins quite by accident, and though she knew I knew, by mutual discretion, neither of us had ever mentioned it. Normally, she made a point of having as little to do with Bernie's writers as possible. Heaven only knew why she made an exception for me.

"I'm so glad you're here. It was very careless of Bernard to allow you to drive up like that, especially in this wretched weather. You must turn your car in here and fly back with us."

Allow? I fought down a bristle of temper.

Charity was not one of Anita's strong points. I could imagine her dismay at being trapped in the small confines of a small chartered plane with several of the people she disliked most. Not even she at her most regal could ignore someone for the entire flight, especially someone as determinedly obnoxious as Clement, who regarded baiting her pretensions almost as an Olympic sport.

It wouldn't do any good to tell her that I was a grown woman, and there was no question of Bernie *'allowing'* me to do anything. I had tried it before, and it had gone right past her unnoticed.

Anita would adore Kevin. If they ever became allies, I would be a gone goose.

"I simply didn't have anyone to talk to," she complained. "You cannot abandon me to them again."

"I had sort of planned to drive through the mountains to Vancouver before flying home…"

"Nonsense. You'll be much too busy polishing your book. Anyway, we can talk about it at tea. I've reserved a table for us at four."

How typical of Anita; no invitation, just a command. I glanced at the bedside clock. It was just now three-thirty.

"Anita, I don't think I can make it…"

"Don't be silly, Elizabeth," she said condescendingly. "Of course you can."

* * *

Of course I could. Without really knowing why I rushed so, I skinned into my new, floor-length floral dress. It had cost the earth and looked more like it belonged on a tropical island instead of at a snowy mountain resort, but if one is going to be an author, one should look like an author, no? After brushing my hair, I decided against a necklace, but chose gaudy, dangly earrings. They looked like chandeliers, so I replaced them with simple pearl drops.

I had lost weight since the dress was fitted, and it hung almost loosely around my hips. The effect wasn't really flattering, and for that I had to thank *Daughters of Passion*.

Anita was waiting for me downstairs. Part of the lobby had been converted into a tearoom by the use of velvet ropes; the old oak tables had been covered with snowy linen cloths. A group of nicely starched youngsters were dispensing tea and cakes. The place was packed, with a line waiting for tables.

Seeing me through the crowd, Anita waved a lazy hand. I picked my way through the tables, which were jammed with duplicates of the giggling crowd in the bar.

"Quite a crowd, isn't there?" I dropped gratefully if ungracefully into a seat. Anita Wingate's elegance had the effect of always making me feel gauche and clumsy.

As usual she was impeccably dressed, this time in an eggplant-colored little wool suit and lace blouse that simply screamed Paris. Next to her I felt tacky and gaudy in my new outfit; thank goodness I had ditched the chandelier earrings.

Compared to the rest of the group we were both fashion plates. I had never seen such a mish-mash of what an ill-assorted group of women considered the proper thing to wear for the occasion. From her expression, neither had Anita.

"Quite. Have you ever seen such atrocious clothes?" Her nostrils quivered slightly as if there were an unpleasant odor instead of the pleasant fragrance of formal tea.

No, I hadn't, and I was working at being charitable. There was everything from mass-market polyester to blue jeans to indescribable things that had to have been homemade by novice seamstresses. The worst thing was that you could just tell every one of those women thought they looked just wonderful.

"And," Anita hissed, pouring me a cup of tea from the squat white pot, "have you ever seen such behavior? They act as if they had never had formal tea before in their lives. Milk?"

I didn't think it prudent to tell her that in a truly

proper service one should put the milk in before pouring the tea. "Please. One sugar." I took the cup and looked around at the group. Housewives. Secretaries. Shop girls. Women hoping to add a little glamour to their lives.

Not everyone is as lucky as you are, my egalitarian little mind preached; *you lead your own life, you are celebrated in your field, you live in a romantic city...*

You are a complete dud when it comes to real romance.

"Probably, they haven't."

Anita sniffed, as if she had been having formal tea every day of her life instead of having to fight to get out of an environment so horrible most people couldn't even imagine it. I wondered at her lack of understanding.

"They should learn."

"I guess." I took a small iced cake from the tray. Sometimes I didn't like Anita very much, and sometimes I didn't like her at all.

"Tell me, how is your book coming?"

Boy, Bernie must really be uptight about *Daughters of Passion* if he had persuaded Anita to talk about it. I had known he was impatient, but this was unprecedented.

"I know I'm behind deadline, but things aren't going too well. I've had this conference on my mind, and then there's Kevin...And it's not like *Sisters of Desire* is going to fade away right quick..."

"No, I didn't mean that rubbish!" Anita made a quick negative gesture. "Heavens, no, I didn't mean any of that quick-money trash Bernard makes you write. I meant your real book...the sequel to *A Woman of Quality.*"

Without meaning to — I think — Anita had hit a nerve. "I haven't been thinking about it recently, if you want the

26

truth. I..."

"Writer's block?" she asked. She hadn't been married to a publisher for years without learning something of the ills that afflict writers.

I nodded.

"It's one of the worst things about having a smash success for your first book. Critical acclaim goes to your head..."

"It didn't go to my head. It was wonderful, but then *A Woman of Quality* was a good book. So good, in fact, I'm afraid I'll never do that well again."

She pinioned me with a cold blue gaze. "So you are content to laze along as Liz Allison and write trash?"

"No, I'm not, but I'm terrified of trying and failing." My words, tumbling out seemingly of their own accord, amazed even me. I had avoided facing the issues for so long, and here I was blurting out everything to Anita Wingate, of all people. "And if I don't get cracking with *Daughters of Passion*, I might..."

"No." Anita set her teacup down with a snap. "Forget that rubbish, and get on with your real work, Elizabeth."

"I have a contract with Bernie..."

"So what? Talent and quality should not be subject to puny things like contracts. It hurts me to see a gift like yours wasted on that vulgar romantic drivel."

"Now who is maligning our bread and butter?"

There was no mistaking that snide drawl. Anita and I looked upward into his thin, avid face. I at least tried to conceal my distaste.

"Hello, Clement."

In his odd, boneless way he insinuated himself into a chair and looked around with glittering eyes. "Hardly the type of crowd one would wish to get used to, is it?"

He had deliberately spoken loud enough for half the room to hear, and not knowing that they bought his books by the thousands, the women understandably turned to give him dirty looks. Even though I had done nothing, I flushed with embarrassment.

"If you cannot behave yourself, Clement, I suggest that you leave."

"Now, don't get on your high ropes, Anita old girl. You don't want to offend one of your dear hubby's highest earners, do you? After all, if I decided to go elsewhere, you might not get that new fur or whatever it is you want."

Anita's eyes were glittering dangerously. Now, I am no saint, nor overly fond of either of them, but I hated to see bloodshed in public, especially in such a beautiful setting. I would not let these two unpleasant brats spoil what little pleasure I was finding here.

"Clement! Behave yourself."

"But, my dear Liz, I have been! I haven't said one of those divinely nasty little four-letter words. Bernie said I mustn't while we're here, though for this crowd I can't see why he would worry," he added in a 'just-us-girls' voice that only carried over half the tea area. Then surprisingly enough he calmed down, taking a sandwich from the plate and eating it in ostentatiously dainty bites. Either he had made the scene he had intended, or he knew just how far he could push Anita. The plane ride must have been hellish for her; Anita-baiting really was one of Clement's joys.

Jealousy sometimes takes strange forms.

"Aren't the mountains beautiful?" I asked determinedly, looking out the arched window at the snowy vista beyond.

Anita picked up her teacup, looked at it as if something loathsome had surfaced from its milky depths and put it down again. Her mouth was a thin, bitter line. "I am glad you, at least, have a sense of what is proper, Elizabeth. I shall see you tonight at the Wingate Publications dinner."

With the grace of an anointed queen, she rose to her full height, and without waiting for an answer, threaded her way out into the lobby towards the elevators. She gave no sign of having heard Clement's sprightly, "Me, too, darling!"

I turned back to the mountains, drinking in their serenity. "Why do you deliberately work at antagonizing her so?"

"I don't." He shrugged and reached for one of the little iced cakes. It was simply infuriating how he could eat constantly and never gain any weight. "I can't help it if she gets antagonized by me being myself."

"That's not what I mean. You go out of your way to goad her. Why?"

He shrugged, something unidentifiable flittering in his eyes. They were the same color as old ice. "She doesn't have to be so damn snooty about what she is…What she wants people to think she is." Abruptly his expression changed and focused hungrily on something behind me. "Lookie, lookie…There goes a delicate tidbit for one of us. Tall and dark-haired...Better make our move fast before these hags start sinking their claws into him."

My fingers tightened around the teacup to keep it from rattling. Despite its heat, my hand was cold. There had been a time, not too long ago, that I had eagerly turned around for every tall, dark-haired man, hoping against hope to see the one I wished.

Even wishes die in time, someone had said. I hoped so.

I didn't even turn around.

"Go on, then. I'll see you tonight."

Clement oozed up out of his seat like a predator and slithered off on the trail of his prey. I almost wished him luck. Someone should be happy.

* * *

There was just long enough of a break before Bernie's cocktail hour for me to run up to my room. Run? Retreat. As soon as Clement left, I could feel the attention of the nearby tables intensifying as the housewives and secretaries tried to decide if I were someone worth approaching or not.

One woman, in brilliantly patterned polyester no one should wear, was braver than the rest. Approaching like a juggernaut, an ominous-looking package clasped to her chest, she smiled hopefully.

"You're Liz Allison, aren't you? May I have your autograph?" Without waiting for an answer, she dug in a cavernous tote bag and pulled out a battered copy of *Sisters of Desire* with the name of an Ohio used bookstore stamped on it.

I took it with distaste, both for the condition and the origin. In spite of popular belief, authors receive only a tiny percent of a book's cover price when it is sold new; they get nothing at all from used book sales. Still, there was nothing to be gained from alienating a potential reader...if I ever published another book. She had a pen, too, which was a refreshing change. I scrawled "Best regards, Liz Allison" on the title page, right under the used bookstore's $.50 price stamp.

"I really enjoyed *Sisters of Desire*, Liz," she said, stuffing the book back into her carryall. The seams groaned. "My book is set in the same time, but in Missouri, not Louisiana. Everyone who's read it says it's as good as yours. Would you give it to your publisher? I know they'll like it and maybe give you a bonus for finding a new best-selling author..."

The thick package, alluringly wrapped in a brown paper grocery bag, hovered dangerously near my nose.

"I'm sorry," I said, ungracefully slithering sideways out of the chair, "but I don't do anything with submissions. Have your agent send it to Wingate in the normal manner."

Propelled by her scrawny hands, the manuscript followed my face. "I don't have an agent," she said in the same strangely condescending tone. "You can give this to yours instead, if you want."

I was past politeness. "No."

"At least you can give me his name...I'll tell him you told me to submit it, so you'll get the credit for discovering me." She was starting to sound exasperated.

"I'm not interested," I called over my shoulder and

tried not run flat out for the elevators. If she followed, would I have to beat her off with my purse?

"Well!" she snorted loudly enough for most of the tea area to hear, returning in defeat to her friends. "See if I ever buy any of her books again!"

* * *

Just as she had probably intended, Anita's words stung. I had brought my old portable typewriter and manuscript notebooks along more as habit and good intentions than from any real inclination to work.

I didn't know why I was having so much trouble with *Daughters of Passion*. The one before, *Sisters of Desire* had gone like cream. I had written all 100,000 words of it in less than two months, and although it had been on the stands a couple of months, it was still selling like wildfire. *Daughters*, the continuation of the saga of the Winterfell clan, was in trouble. I had been working on it for almost three months and still had less than 10,000 words.

Bernie had a reason to be upset.

Flopping across the bed, I picked up the scribbled-over manuscript of *Daughters of Passion* and studied it. Trash.

Trash!

The printed part was bad enough, but the handwritten additions only made it worse. The tortured words read like the worst effusions of a particularly stupid tyro trying to write her first novel. Even that bad-mannered cow downstairs could probably write better. Well...*maybe* she could.

From critical acclaim to this. I felt like weeping.

Burnt out, used up, no good...

And I had the temerity to try and teach those sincere, aspiring writers downstairs. Rather, Bernie had had the temerity to tell me I would.

I ripped the pages from the notebook, tore them very neatly into quarters and threw them away.

The other notebook lay quietly on the desk. I handled it as gently as if it had been an active bomb.

A Man of Honor

I looked the manuscript over slowly, horrified at how yellow and dog-eared the pages were. Surely it hadn't been that long since I had worked with it. I hadn't ignored it until it had started to die!

One by one I turned the pages, vaguely impressed that I could ever have written so well. This was music compared to what was on the torn-up pages in the wastebasket; the cadence of the words intrigued me. I wondered if I could ever write that way again.

The prospect was depressing in the extreme. It was not any more cheering to see that it was almost time for Bernie's little conclave. I freshened my make-up, and feeling rather like Marie Antoinette on the way to the guillotine, went downstairs. Old Marie, however, knew what awaited her; I could never have dreamed...

Chapter Three

The bar was crowded. It seemed every minute there were more women checking in for the conference, and the biggest part of the attendees weren't expected until the next day. The thing didn't even start until the formal tea tomorrow night, and there weren't any workshops until the day after. What were they finding to talk about? I walked slowly through the crowded tables to the corner Bernie had appropriated and listened.

To anyone who didn't know the purpose of this gathering the conversation must have been startling. In that short walk through the bar area, I heard fragments of a seduction aboard a ship, a proposal in a rose garden, a seduction in a stables, a duel in the bayous, a seduction out on the moors, a girl who rose from the perfume counter to the presidency of a multinational corporation, a seduction in a rose garden, a proposal on a ship in the moonlight...

By the time I reached Bernie's table I was feeling rather shell-shocked.

"Liz, my dear, I'm so glad you could come," Bernie said just as if I had had a choice in the matter. Standing to his full five-feet-six, he leaned over the table and bussed me on the cheek. Jane nodded, which was just about as much as she ever did, and Anita, hovering by Bernie's side as she always did, gave me an unexpectedly warm smile.

The only seat left was one with its back to the room,

which suited me just fine. I'd much rather watch the fading scenery anyway. There was still a little light in the sky, though not enough to show much beyond the small perimeter of the hotel's scenic spotlights. The vista had become a study in black and white, vaguely reminiscent of some of Ansel Adams's later work. Glowing with the last light of the departing sun, the mountains stood like sentinels around the frozen lake, which in some eerie way, seemed to emanate a light of its own.

"Liz, see if you can talk some sense into this man," purred Vanessa. Her hat was gone now, and somehow, she had sobered up remarkably. Now, like everyone else, she was sipping champagne, which Bernie insisted was her avowed drink of choice, at least when there were fans present. This afternoon she must have been really stressed out to drink anything else.

Or thirsty.

"Sense?"

She gestured toward the crowded bar. "This is no place for a meeting. It's so crowded and all those staring tourists...The least you could have done, Bernie, is get a private room for us."

Bernie looked up, but his eyes lacked the customary twinkle they usually had when he was discussing finances. "Vanessa, all those tourists buy books, Wingate Publications books. One of the reasons they come to these conferences is to see their favorite authors. They can't see you if we're in a private room." The words were soft, but their message was unmistakable. Bernie could be quite charming, but he was first and foremost a businessman.

"Just like a zoo exhibit," Clement murmured to no

one in particular.

Vanessa flushed and chugged her champagne. Bernie poured a tiny splash into her glass, and then poured me a full one.

"It would seem," she said in a bright voice as glittery as ice, "that our dear Liz is thoroughly bemused by those mountains,"

"I can't see why," Clement said. He had a habit of keeping the drink stirrers arranged in front of him as a counter. Although he was now drinking champagne, there were a fair number heaped up, and I wondered if he had been drinking since we had parted.

"We don't have anything like this in New Orleans. Aren't they just magnificent?"

Clement threw a quick, dismissive glance outside. "They just look like a lot of big tits to me."

Vanessa slammed her empty glass down on the table as her perfectly arranged features crumpled with anger. Anita's face didn't change, not really, it just sort of froze into a mask of distaste, and then she leaned over and hissed something in Bernie's ear.

Embarrassed, I looked down at my hands. I needed a manicure desperately; my nails were chewed ragged. Better handle that before the conference started. Women noticed such things.

Of all of us, only Jane was nonplussed. She sipped at her nearly full glass and then daintily dabbed at her lips with the tiny napkin. She didn't even leave any lipstick smears on it.

"Clement," Bernie said slowly, "don't you think...?"

Shrugging, Clement looked away. "I know. Behave

myself. None of you are any fun at all."

For a moment there was an uneasy silence among us, broken only by a slight trilling from the piano as if someone were warming up. I stiffened instinctively, then—vertebra by vertebra—made myself relax. I had seen the piano there earlier in the afternoon. It only stood to reason that sooner or later someone would play it. Didn't everyone warm up by running arpeggios? I took a deep breath. I couldn't spend my entire life avoiding pianos.

Clearing his throat ostentatiously, Bernie lifted his glass. "To Wingate Publications."

We all toasted obediently.

"This is a special day in the life of Wingate Publications," Bernie went on. I would swear that his eyes were moist, the sentimental old thing. "It is now four years since we published our first genre romance, and in that time our gross profits have doubled, trebled, quadrupled...and with writers like you, there's no end in sight. By next year we should be seriously challenging the big boys. I drink to you..."

Behind me the piano erupted into a flowery version of "It Might As Well Be Spring"—a rather sarcastic choice, I thought, considering the snow outside. It also sounded like whoever was playing it wanted to make sure not one note was overlooked.

"...all of you. First to you, Jane Hall, for bringing us your tremendous talent when we were a struggling fledgling in this field..."

"And your tremendous following," muttered the irrepressible Clement under his breath. Jane acknowledged the toast with a brief little nod.

"...and then to you, Clement Wallingford, for your versatility..."

Clement preened. The florid piano music swelled and shrank with tide-like regularity.

"...and then to you, Vanessa Mangold, for your presence and your infallible sense of the romantic..."

"And those dreadful flowered hats you wear at speeches," Clement hissed in my ear while Vanessa cooed and fluttered.

"...and lastly to you, Liz Allison, for daring to take a risk and switch fields. I salute you all, for you are the backbone of...Wingate Romances!"

"Wingate Romances!" Vanessa cried as joyously as a girl. She even clapped her hands together in a gesture that had been old in the days of silent movies. "So you're really going to do it."

My gaze snapped to Anita; her face was as hard and shiny as wax. Bernie had been talking about changing the name of the company for some time, but judging from Anita's frozen reaction, he hadn't told her he was really going to do it. I didn't envy him tonight.

"Yes, I've decided it is for the best. We can phase out the trade and literature books and triple our romance output each month. I'm looking for all of you to recruit us some really good talent during this conference..."

Clement leered as he deliberately misunderstood. He licked his lips with an oddly reptilian motion. "I always try, dear boy..."

The song changed to a rippling version of "Someone to Watch Over Me". I bit my lips. It seemed like the pianist was intent on giving us a sample of all the old romantic chestnuts. Once I had heard a parody of that same song, which had sounded very much like that, all rippling crescendos and sugary harmonies.

It had seemed funny then.

Vanessa glanced over her shoulder, and then leaned forward conspiratorially. In her ruffled pink dress, she looked like something that should be sitting on top of a cheap cake. I had felt sort of gaudy compared to Anita's chic little suit and Jane Hall's boring basic black, but next to Vanessa's rosy magnificence, no one would notice me.

"You know that Harcourt man is here from Peters and Worcester."

"Of course. You didn't think he, or any of the other editors, would miss a meeting like this. They're setting up appointments to see the new writers, just like the agents are. Just like Bernie is."

Business bored Clement, probably since he couldn't fantasize about it. After Vanessa had turned her attention to obtaining a fresh bottle of champagne, he leaned over to whisper in my other ear.

"I'm afraid I'm out of the running for that gorgeous hunk."

Jane Hall's voice entered the conversation like a drift of windblown sand. "How big of a first run are you planning?"

"Hunk?" I asked.

Bernie pulled a folded paper from his pocket. He loved to talk figures and projections, totaling up all the money he planned to make. He usually made it, too. "I thought we'd hold with a fifty thousand initial run..."

Janis Susan May

"I don't see why you must discontinue printing quality books completely, Bernard."

"I do," Bernie answered shortly. "They take too much work and don't make enough money."

Her face rigid, Anita sipped at her champagne and focused her gaze far past us.

"That dark-haired Adonis in the lobby."

"Oh."

"What about the length requirements?" Jane asked, her eyes devouring the projection sheets.

"Anyway, I did some checking and it turns out he's lamentably straight." Clement sighed dramatically. "What a waste. I never have any luck. You'd better get busy before all these romantic-minded harpies get in before you. Seems women just can't resist a piano player."

How well I knew!

Once, as a child, I had experienced a premonition of danger which had proved to be true; I had shivered as cold waves had lapped at my nerves and my grandmother, noticing my reaction, had said, 'That's a ghost walking over your grave." That phrase had always seemed so sinister to me, so tied in with fear and premonitions come true; it was so now, for instantly I knew—*I knew* – what was happening.

I knew who sat behind me, and I knew that the fragile new life I had built for myself was going to be changed forever.

As if in answer to my thoughts, the melody changed again, this time flowing into a sugary version of "Why Do I Love You?" My neck felt as if it had rusted solid. I had to force it to turn.

There were at least three tables crowded with chattering women between us, but I had no trouble recognizing him. I could have recognized him all the way across Central Park. Even though I couldn't see them from where I sat, I knew how his long, thin hands—true musicians' hands—were moving over the keys with a lightness that belied their incredible strength.

I had watched them often enough.

He hadn't seen me. From the look of glazed boredom in his eyes, I would have guessed that he wasn't seeing much of anything. I turned back around and took a long gulp of champagne, wishing it were something stronger. It seemed that no one had noticed anything, that there were no bells or sirens or earthquakes except in me.

"I was thinking of having three different lengths," Bernie was saying with the enthusiasm he always had for one of his ideas. I made myself concentrate on each word. "Keep the long ones, up to 150,000 words, and the category length, 50,000 to 60,000 words, but add a shorter line...novella length, 25,000 to 40,000."

Jane frowned. "But no one is buying those."

"No publisher, at least, not now. I think the public will go for them, though. There are times when a long book or even a category length is too much. Think of airports and doctors' waiting rooms and places like that. Keep them short, keep them cheap and sell lots of them." Bernie's eyes were sparkling.

Clement looked back over his shoulder. "Nice, huh? His name is Jerry Grant."

"How many would you want in the pipeline?"

Jerry Grant?

"Do you think you could have three ready by...say, August?"

"At 35,000 words each, easily."

"Now Liz, you can never say your Uncle Clement never did anything for you, but if you find a nice tidbit wandering around, I do expect you to reciprocate." He chuckled lewdly.

"So could I," Vanessa announced. "Do you want contemporary or historical?"

"I think contemporary to start with...don't you?"

"Definitely," said Jane Hall. Of course, she only wrote contemporaries.

Clement and I were silent; each for our own reasons, but no one seemed to notice.

"If you could get us a manuscript by next month, we could rush up production and possibly get into the stores by mid-July...maybe pick up the late vacation crowd..." Bernie was alive with temptation.

"Will you do a test market or simply announce?" There was a hint of sparkle in Jane's eyes, and she looked more animated than I had ever seen her. Perhaps beneath the negligible breast of that prolific romantic novelist did beat the stolid heart of a CPA.

"I think we'll just announce and release the next month. Give it a big publicity push; call them mini-books or something."

"You could always call them quickies," Clement said brightly.

The music, now something lush that I didn't

recognize, flowed through the air as thick and as cloying as molten fudge. You could almost strangle in it.

The last time I had seen him, he had been sitting at a piano, too. It had been at Carnegie Hall, his last concert there, and his name had not been Jerry Grant.

I had been foolish enough to go, insisting against the protests of friends that I had to go, that it wouldn't hurt me. I had sat up in the gods, way back up in the highest seats where I could barely see, let alone be seen. It was quite a change from the front row seat I had always occupied before, the seat then filled by my replacement.

He had given an all Chopin program that night, finishing with — painfully enough — my favorite, the "Piano Concerto Number 2 in F Minor, op. 21". That he was playing my favorite of all the repertoire had seemed cruel at the time, even though I knew those things were set months in advance.

"Bernie!" Vanessa squealed, pointedly ignoring Clement. "You can't. 'Mini' is such a vulgar catchphrase. It's so over-used..."

"Just think how many more books you two can write, darlings," Clement purred poisonously. "All that money you can make..."

Jane shot him a withering glance. "At least I haven't lost my touch."

That stung Clement. He hadn't had a book out in almost six months — an enormous amount of time considering his past track record — and a nasty rumor had been flying that he had dried up permanently. His face went even more deadly white than usual and then flushed an ugly red. "Bitch!"

With admirable grace Anita stepped into the tense situation. Lifting her glass she spoke softly, but with a voice that carried an unmistakable edge. "Since Bernard sprung it on us so unexpectedly, we were all unprepared to acknowledge the company's name change. I am sure it will make a great deal of money. To Wingate Romances."

We all drank a rather fervent toast. I for one was glad of the diversion, and my admiration for Anita increased. She wouldn't be sitting here cringing just because some guy was playing the piano...

I signaled the waitress. "Miss, could you please ask the pianist for something a little more classical? Perhaps..." Metaphorically I took my courage in my hands. "...some Chopin?"

Of course the others ribbed me a little about my new taste for classical music, but I didn't mind. They didn't know. This had all come after...

"Ma'am?" The pert little waitress was back almost instantly. "Mr. Grant said he was sorry, but he didn't know anything by Chopin." She pronounced it 'Show-pan.'

Talk about a put-down! I glanced over my shoulder again; I don't know why. There was no way I could have been mistaken. Perhaps...Heck! It wasn't my problem any more. He had made that abundantly clear over two years before. I had handled my problem.

"Better drink up, gang," Bernie said, in example, draining his champagne as if it were soda. "I've got a table reserved up in the Empress Room. Tonight we celebrate."

* * *

As far as celebrations went, it was a dud. The dining room was a monument to *fin-de-siecle* elegance, with marble and white linen and shining silver all inside red-flocked walls. Only the steak knives were modern and prosaic with their stainless steel blades and wooden handles. I didn't pay much attention to them then, no one did, not until later, when no one could ignore them. At the time we were intent on our dinner — which was excellent — and the party — which was miserable.

Jane and Anita determinedly kept up a desultory chatter about some book function they had attended in New York. Vanessa babbled continually about the place of the romance novel in American life, stressing the necessity of traditional values of home, family and fidelity. Bernie agreed with her, but his stress was more on the available market and how much of it Wingate Romances could corner. Clement was sulking ostentatiously, waiting for someone to draw him out and coax him into ribald good humor again; he was also getting angrier by the minute because no one either dared or cared. It was hard to decide which could be more tiresome — Clement in high grig, or Clement in high dudgeon.

And I? I tried to force myself back into the place I had been earlier, tried to pretend that revelation in the bar had never been made.

I failed miserably.

The gates of memory had been hard to shut, but once opened again, they were impossible to close. While I quietly agreed with Vanessa about romance being a force for good, I was remembering calm walks in Central Park and acrimonious quarrels. That was the trouble with memories; you could never select just the good or the bad. They all came tumbling out mixed up together, and you had to take them as they came.

Anita noticed my distraction and mentioned it. I answered—quite truthfully—that I was thinking about something, and they accepted it. Other writers and people who work with writers are quite accustomed to us going off inside our heads for a while. Finally, Clement, convinced that no one was going to play his little game, re-entered the conversation in as subdued and proper a manner as even Anita could wish.

At last it was over, and I think everyone was as glad as I. Someone suggested a nightcap in the bar. While the others were discussing it, I said my hurried goodnights and tried not to run as I left.

It was the last time we were all together. I still wonder if I had stayed just a little longer if I could have prevented the horror that followed.

* * *

It was snowing. It wasn't the dirty, swirling grayness I remembered from New York, but rather, a perfect, fairyland kind of snow. Huge white flakes drifted down, almost in slow motion, to settle like lacy-winged butterflies. I wrapped my arms around me and watched with hypnotic fascination. Living in the tropics had its points, but it offered nothing like this.

I knew it was very late. Most of the lights in the hotel were out, and the little elevator girl who had brought me down had been more asleep than awake. After leaving the others, I had gone up to my room and prepared for bed; then, more to keep my mind occupied than through any desire to work, I had sat down with *A Man of Honor*.

In a way it had been depressing, but it had been exhilarating, too. As I read, fragments of plans, of thoughts, of ideas came back; words began forming sentences in my mind, wonderful sentences that would say just what I had in mind. Flushed with enthusiasm, I dug out the typewriter and rolled in a fresh sheet of paper.

Twenty minutes later I was back on the bed, staring at the ceiling. The elegant sentences that had formed so easily in my head would not transfer to paper; they snarled, they tangled, they knotted into impenetrable lumps of adjectives that nothing would straighten. I had forgotten the sweat it took to get a decent thought into words. The effort was too much right now.

In spite of being charming, my room became unbearable. It was cheerily decorated in yellow stripes and French provincial furniture, but it was small. Set just off a tiny hallway, mine was one of three rooms that formed a buttress-like bay on the lakeside of the hotel. Outside my one big window, there was a vast expanse of darkness sprinkled with drifting snow. It was irresistible.

Slipping into jeans, a sweater and my sturdy old mink jacket—reclaimed from two years of cold storage specifically for this trip—I had crept through the quiet hotel. Aside from the smooth whoosh of the elevator, the only sound in the dimly lit lobby was a tinny echo of canned music coming up the stairs from some lower level. Probably there were conferees still partying down there, but I didn't want to join them.

I had gone quietly outside onto the promenade and followed the steps down to the lake. Although a few of the exterior floods were still on, it was much dimmer out here. The lake itself and the path which followed its shore were in complete darkness, as was the sky. From this view one couldn't tell if there were any mountains around or not. I couldn't even see the snowman out on the lake.

"Hello."

I didn't even bother to turn around. Had this been why I had come out so late? Was this a last-gasp manifestation of the closeness we had once shared, some vestige of the unspoken communication all couples had, telling me he would be here? Normally I wasn't night-restless.

Had I hoped to meet him?

"Hello, Jared."

"I thought that might be you in the bar tonight. I didn't see you until you were leaving, and even then, I wasn't sure. You were the one who asked for Chopin, weren't you?"

I could see him now. He had walked up into the light from the shadow of a grove of trees off to the side. Despite a few more wrinkles and an almost invisible scar on his forehead, his features hadn't really changed; his eyes were still dark and hooded, his mouth full and surprisingly sensuous on such a hawkish face.

On closer examination, though, there was something indefinably different about him; the fire was gone from his once brilliant eyes. There were deep lines on either side of his mouth. Even in this light a faint dusting of silver showed in his wavy black mane. Obviously the last two and a half years had not been good ones. He looked older, harder, bitterer.

I suppose I did, too.

"Yes, as soon as I recognized you."

"That wasn't kind."

"I didn't..." I began then stopped. Had I meant it to wound? I didn't know.

"I'd like to have seen your face when the waitress told you I didn't know any Chopin." A brief, bitter smile flirted with the corners of his mouth and then faded. "Of course, I didn't know it was you then."

"It was a surprise. What's this Jerry Grant bit, Jared?"

He shrugged and leaned against a pole. "The name Jared Granville was a little notorious there for a while."

"The accident. I know." It was a chore to keep my voice level. I had read the grisly details, as had most of the country, and if I had grieved irrationally that I had not been the one to die beside him...well, that was no one's business but my own. "I didn't mention it to anyone."

Following the abrupt change of subject with ease, he looked at me with some surprise. He was still very handsome. "I didn't think you would."

"Well, our parting was..."

"Hateful."

"Nasty."

"I..." He began, and then silence fell between us, thicker and more deadly than the drifting snow.

There seemed to be nothing more to say, so we stood

there for a while watching the snow fall. Odd. I had pictured our meeting again over and over and over. In my fantasies it had been sometimes passionate, sometimes acrimonious, but never silent. It was incredible, but we had nothing to say.

Finally, he asked, "What are you doing here?"

"The 'Just Write for Love Conference'. Didn't you think...?" I stopped. Of course not; we had long been over before Bernie had talked me into writing a romance.

"Are you doing romances now?"

"For a while. Just to keep me going until I can finish *A Man of Honor*."

"I read *A Woman of Quality*. It was very good."

Coming from him, that was a tremendous concession. "Thank you."

"Will you be here long?"

"Three or four days. Until the end of the conference for sure. Then I thought I'd drive over to Vancouver, see a little of this part of the world. Have you been here long?" I asked tentatively, suddenly bubbling over with questions. From one of the most lionized, up-and-coming concert pianists to a hack playing syrupy cocktail piano in a remote Canadian resort; how had it happened? How did he—he of the damnable, stiff-necked pride—stand it?

"About a month. I'm booked through the end of May. I was in Vegas before that." He said it matter-of-factly, as if telling me he had eaten corned beef for lunch. The Jared Granville I had known would never have said anything so simply, especially something damaging to his pride. "That looks like your old jacket."

"It is." He had been the one who bought it for me. "It

doesn't get any use back home. I had to get it out of storage."

"You moved back to New Orleans?"

"East or west, home's best." The flippancy was out of place, and I was sorry for having said it. Still, a part of me wept that he had not even had the curiosity to find out where I had gone. Blast the man!

"You always liked that part of the country."

Suddenly, I was very cold and not only from the thickening snow. There was nothing deader than the ashes of an old love. Perhaps that wasn't a very original observation, but things are always fresh when you discover them for yourself. "At least it's warmer."

He glanced up at the sky. "Looks like we're in for a good one. That snow's really coming down. We'd best go in. Can I walk you to the hotel?"

"If you're going that way. Are you staying in the hotel?"

"No. The staff lives up at Hillside House. That way."

"I won't take you out of your way, then." Although my body still tingled to treacherous memories of his embraces, I forestalled any potential attempt by extending my hand as if to the most casual of acquaintances. "Good-bye, Jared."

We shook hands with remote formality. I started up the walk, now slippery with sticking snow and didn't look back.

"Floor, miss?" asked the elevator girl. She didn't look sleepy now.

"Two, please."

Maybe it sounds sybaritic to take an elevator to the

second floor; that's what I thought until I had climbed it earlier in the afternoon and found that the Canadians followed the British system of having a ground floor, with floors one and two and so forth above that. The climb to my second floor room was up three very long flights of stairs.

"Was that Mr. Grant you were talking to, Miss?"

"Yes," I answered automatically, too wrapped up in my own turmoil to notice her avidity until it was too late.

"Lucky you! Isn't he just the dishiest thing you've ever seen? Every girl on the staff is just gaga over him."

I had forgotten the effect that Jared's moody, Byronic looks had on impressionable females. He would be positively besieged by the time the conference was over, poor thing. I felt sorry for him.

"He seems very nice," I said repressively.

She seemed disappointed that I didn't say more. I couldn't. I felt empty, desiccated, bereft.

Tonight I had lost Jared so much more than I had two and a half years ago.

Chapter Four

I didn't sleep well that night. It wasn't all my emotions; I refuse to be counted as such a weakling. About two, the wind began to blow, a wind like I'd never heard before. It started after I was asleep, but my sleep was restless, and I was conscious of the unholy howling that raged at my window. The only comparable sound I could think of was when New Orleans huddled under the lashing of a hurricane.

Finally, the clamor pulled me into full wakefulness. It was like no awakening I had ever had before. Even though it was well before seven, my room was filled with a glowing, cold white light.

Beyond the window, where yesterday there had been trees and rocks and walks, there was now nothing but a curtain of unbroken white. Snow covered everything. Snow filled the sky, swirling in a perpetual cloud that was as solid as anything below.

A blizzard...

With the tropic-dweller's unthinking delight in such phenomena, I opened the window and reached out into the whirling mass, gasping at the physical blow of the cold wind. I slammed the window shut and dived under the covers, seeking the warm spot where I had lain. The frilly cotton gown I wore was no match for a blizzard.

A blizzard. My mind began to work. This would surely make a mess of the conference. There was no way anyone could get here in this, and most of the conferees weren't supposed to arrive until today.

Conversely, that meant we couldn't get out.

Being something of a claustrophobe, for a moment I felt a heart-stopping rush of irrational panic, and then the humor of the situation struck. Snowbound in Canada in an elegant resort hotel...if I couldn't get some sort of a story out of this, I should turn in my pencil and become a plumber.

I became more rational as I dressed. Perhaps this wasn't really a blizzard, just a snowstorm, and the people who lived here wouldn't think much of it. Probably, things would be delayed a bit, but they would go on as always. People here were use to the snow. There was nothing unusual going on.

* * *

Somehow in the early morning, the hotel seemed different. Feeling caged in the small room, I decided to explore. It was still early enough that nearly everyone was still asleep. Although there was an eerie white light outside, it didn't penetrate into the building. Most of the lights were on, giving the lobby the artificial look of a stage set waiting to be used.

Only the elevator girls and the busboys were stirring; they regarded my presence with curious eyes. I wandered without purpose, exploring without real curiosity. In the odd white light the rooms seemed bigger, colder...

No, they were colder, definitely colder. I had worn a sweater and skirt that were winter clothes at home, but they were inadequate against the dull chill that seeped into my bones. Fighting back a shiver, I thought about going back up to my room for heavy slacks and another sweater and decided against it. Probably the heating was just turned down in the public rooms. When the guests started stirring the management would turn up the thermostat.

The first floor (the second as far as I was concerned) was ornate. Besides the opulent Empress dining room, there was a sprinkling of elegant shops, a room mercifully closed off with soundproof doors for a bank of pinball machines, which I thought utterly incongruous in this elegant setting, and directly overlooking the lake, a writing room that was right out of a Victorian novel. Little desks with leather pads and hotel stationery sat in front of the huge windows so that guests could sit and write their letters home. Did anyone write letters anymore? Somehow I felt those desks hadn't seen anything but postcards for years.

Behind double doors beyond the medical facilities (open only during the ski season) was the stairway down to the swimming pool. The pool itself was on the ground floor, set in a large room with walls made mainly of glass. It looked to be Olympic-sized, and clouds of steam hung thickly over it.

On the other side of the pool, the steam was thicker over the deep end of the pool. I'm not a particularly good swimmer, but I love splashing about in the water. This would be a good place to remember if things at the conference got to be too much to handle...and if everyone else didn't discover it too. The idea of trying to relax in a pool full of aspirant writers like the one yesterday was horrifying.

Finally, all the way down on the lowest level, I found what I had really been seeking—the coffee shop. And, thank the gods that may be, it was open. I didn't even mind that it had no windows.

Two cups of excellent coffee later, my outlook on life and the world in general was much improved. The waitress was a cheery young thing who paused only long enough to fill my cup before dashing back to the corner where she giggled continually with a handsome boy in a bellman's uniform. I felt good seeing them. After laboring for so many months with manufactured romance, love by the word count, passion by the pound, it was nice to know that simple boy-girl attraction still existed.

It was eight-fifteen. At eight-thirty all the participating speakers had been scheduled to meet in the Empress. Despite the warming coffee, I was still cold down to my bones. Style or no, I was going to get warm. There was just enough time to run upstairs and put on my slacks and a heavy sweater. For once I was grateful that writers had the reputation of being eccentric.

Even though I hurried I was still late, but the meeting hadn't started yet. The big dining room was frigid and uncomfortably dim. The heavy drapes had been pulled against the whirling whiteness outside, but the lights didn't seem to be as bright as they had been the night before. There was a crowd around the steaming coffee urn, the Danish pastries and doughnuts had already gone cold, and there was an uneasy feeling in the room.

The crowd wasn't that big; there were only fifteen or

so speakers scheduled for the conference, but they had been joined by perhaps half that many agents and editors and maybe a dozen or so organizers and other people.

"I don't know about you, but I'm freezing," said the woman next to me in the crush around the coffee urn. She was probably ten years older than I, thin and short. She also might have had 'I'm from New York' on a sign hung around her neck. "Stupidest thing I ever heard of to have a conference in snow country in the spring."

I agreed wholeheartedly. We edged one layer closer to the coffee table. It was steaming visibly, as was my breath.

"You're Liz Allison with Wingate, aren't you? I'm Winifred MacDougal...I've just taken over as editor-in-chief at Heart's Beat Romances."

I had heard of her. According to Bernie, she was nothing less than an apprentice Witch of Endor, but that was probably just because she had made some very cutting remarks about him at the last ABA luncheon. Of course, there were some who thought such disparagement deserved, especially after, during her assistant editor days, Bernie had noisily and publicly fired her as an (his words, not mine) 'idiotic incompetent who couldn't spell cat without a dictionary.'

Having read some of Heart's Beat's new releases, I was a little inclined to agree with him. However, they sold exceedingly well and were adding two new series, each with monthly releases—'Proper Passion', an old-fashioned Regency line, and 'Working Girl', a series about finding love on the job, usually with the boss.

"I heard about your promotion. Congratulations."

"Is it true that Bernie is going to start publishing nothing but romances?"

I hesitated only a minute. Bernie hadn't said anything about secrecy, and he had been discussing it openly in the bar. "Yes. It's now Wingate Romances."

Winifred shrugged, then rubbed her upper arms and shivered, in spite of the fact she was wearing ski pants and two sweaters. "I knew it had to happen. Everyone jumps on the bandwagon eventually. Are you going to stay with him?"

The question, I feared, would be whether Bernie would want to keep me or not. At the moment I felt as if I would never be able to write another word. "Yes. Bernie gave me my chance."

"Listen to me, Liz," she said coldly, "loyalty isn't always profitable. Sometimes you can advance only laterally. I'd be more than happy to talk to you about a multi-book contract...and you can bet both the advances and the terms would be better that whatever Bernie can offer you."

"Thanks for the offer, but..."

We had reached the coffee urn. She poured two and handed me one. They steamed like dry ice. "It could be a good career move for you. Publishing is a rough business. You never know who's going to survive or not."

I shivered, despite the steaming cup in my hand. This time it had nothing to do with the cold. Even though they were cold, I picked up a cheese Danish. "That sounds like a threat."

Winifred smiled, and it transformed her face. "I wish

it were; I wish I had the guts to make a threat like that and be able to give that ruthless old bastard what he deserves, but I don't. I'm just a simple editor who publishes romance novels. No, what I said was the simple truth, and you've been in the business long enough to know it."

"I'm sorry..."

"No apology necessary. If you change your mind, the door's always open. We can talk later if you like."

Would she keep that door open if she knew how my writing was going? I thought not.

Bernie's group was in the corner furthest from the windows. Anita was swathed in her long fur coat, holding it tightly up around her neck. Her face was pale either from anger or cold, and judging from her expression, I would have bet it was anger, while Bernie's was glowing a dangerous red. Clement and Vanessa had their backs to me, but they were both huddled in their coats.

"I think it is dreadful!" Anita was saying as I joined them. From the others' expressions it was not the first time she had said it.

"What, Anita?"

She hit me with a withering glance. "Everything!"

"What? The snow?"

"The blizzard," Bernie snapped with scant patience. Then he swore, something he rarely did. What was even more telling was that Anita did not reprimand him.

So this really was a blizzard. And, judging from the whirling whiteness outside, it was going to get worse before it ended.

"Don't tell me...the heating plant has gone off?" I gnawed unenthusiastically on the Danish. It felt as if it had come straight from a refrigerator.

"Right."

"But the lights are going...and the coffee pots..."

Clement looked positively morose. With his lugubrious expression and the strange light, he looked almost cadaverous. "There's an emergency generator of sorts, but—surprise, surprise—it appears not to be working too well."

"It's criminal, I say," complained Vanessa to the world in general. Like Anita, she was wearing a glorious coat of some dark fur I didn't recognize. It seemed that she couldn't get far enough inside it. She was probably freezing; her trademark garden-party style dresses weren't meant for anything but ideal temperatures, and I couldn't see her owning anything as prosaic as a sweater. "Someone should do something."

"They will, Vanessa dearest, just as soon as it warms up."

"That's not funny, Clement!" Anita snapped. "Look, there's Gilda Wilcox. She should be able to tell us something."

The crowd parted as the small, dark woman headed toward the speaker's platform. A writer of moderate success who specialized in career romances, Mrs. Wilcox was the spearhead behind this conference. Not only did she do most of the organizing and managing, in the last six months she also finished two books and took care of a large family while she did it. I was in total awe of her.

"May I have your attention, please?" Her voice

boomed out over the loudspeaker, punctuated by a shrill whistle. She moved back a bit and spoke more normally, eyeing the microphone as if it were a hostile organism. "I am sorry to tell you that, due to the weather, we must postpone the conference at least a day. Most of you know that the majority of conferees were due in today. I've just talked by radio with the Mounties down at the station on the highway, and they say that the airport is closed, and Highway 1 is completely impassable. They hope to have everything cleared as soon as possible after the snow stops."

A general groan swept over the assembly, followed almost immediately by a babble of complaint. Everyone had to do something, to be somewhere, and each said so loudly, as if whatever was awaiting them were an irrevocable indicator of their status.

"Please, ladies and gentlemen, please!" Mrs. Wilcox was under strain, and the sound system shrieked again. Despite the frigid room there was a sprinkling of perspiration on her upper lip, and her voice was tight. I didn't blame her. I wouldn't want this group of people mad at me, as if they thought the weather could be controlled by the conference chairman.

"May I have your attention, please...Please!" Gradually the roar died down, and she could speak normally. "Now I'm sure all of you are aware of the power outage and the inadequacy of the emergency generator. The manager assures me that the emergency generator is capable of supplying all the power we need, and he has men working to bring it up to full capacity right now."

A buzz went through the crowd. They were being placated, just as she had intended.

"Now, as to the conference. We really don't know what to do. Less than one quarter of the registered attendees are here. I imagine the rest are stuck somewhere *en route*. It has been suggested that we proceed as scheduled, but since the delay has been called by the weather, that would be dreadfully unfair to the others. I suggest we table that question until this afternoon when we have a better idea of what the weather is going to do. Now, if you'll excuse me, I must go speak to the others."

I sipped morosely at the rapidly cooling coffee. Well, at least I didn't have to be anywhere or do anything at any certain time, and the conference was paying my expenses.

It could be worse, I thought, and the gods laughed.

"I told that Wilcox woman it was too early for this part of the country, but she said the rates were so low now she couldn't ignore them..." Bernie growled. He hated it when his advice was ignored. "Now, there's this damned storm."

"Dreadful!" Anita repeated, as if a persistent enough complaint would make the Almighty rescind His decision to make it snow.

"Isn't it, though?"

Everyone stared as if a rattlesnake had been thrown at their feet. I'm being too harsh; Ralph Harcourt wasn't quite in the rattlesnake class, but no one with any sense would turn their back on him. He had made a career of stealing writers and assistant editors and in doing so had made Peters and Worcester a publishing power around the world. It didn't hurt that he was tall and had more than a passing resemblance to Cary Grant. A resemblance, I might add, that he cultivated assiduously.

"Harcourt," Bernie acknowledged and gave him a quick handshake. The rest of us made do with frosty nods. Ralph Harcourt had, at one time or another, tried to work on all of us and apparently left the same bad impression.

"And how are you this morning, fair Liz?"

Once, in a weak moment, I had gone out to dinner with him, a mistake in judgment Ralph had never let me forget.

"I'm cold, Ralph, just like everyone else."

"But what's cold can be heated up," he said with unpleasant suggestiveness.

Bernie glowered. "Stolen any writers yet, Harcourt?"

"Now, would I steal a writer who didn't really want to be stolen?" His smile was a prototype of unjustly maligned innocence.

Not surprisingly, Clement loathed a hyperactive heterosexual male. Taking full advantage of his superior inches he fixed Ralph with a baleful stare. "That has never stopped you before."

"And it probably never will, but right now I'm making it a priority to rescue 'The Fabulous Four' from Wingate...Romances, isn't it now?"

Apparently grapevines flourished even in the cold.

Ralph made it sound a lighthearted romp to lure away his competitor's authors; I had no doubt he was deadly serious. If he could get any one of us to switch to

Peters and Worcester it would sure be a gold star and a big raise for him.

"We are expanding our operations, yes," Bernie said tightly.

"Just remember kiddies, outside the Bible, a David almost never topples a Goliath." He gave a slick smile that encompassed us all. "I must be going. I've got an appointment, and it just wouldn't do to be late...I'll be talking to you later," he said in a portentous aside to me.

"Where's Jane?" Bernie asked suddenly. "She's not here."

"Isn't she?" Anita looked around quickly, as if expecting to see Jane hiding in some corner.

"Well, I'm here, so you don't have to worry that she's with me," Ralph said, his ears metaphorically pricking. If Jane Hall were not with her publisher when she was supposed to be, and she wasn't with him, where was she?

Or, the horrible thought crept through my mind on clawed little feet, *were the rumors true, and she was his appointment?*

"I haven't seen her this morning," Clement drawled. "At least, I don't think so. With dear Jane you can't always remember."

It was true, but he really didn't have to say it that way.

Vanessa looked around the room. "She's usually so prompt."

"Maybe she overslept," I said, stepping away from Ralph's hand that lingered with uncomfortable intimacy under my elbow.

"More likely she wrote a book last night and is typing it up before breakfast."

"Don't be such a witch, Clement."

"My dear Vanessa, you really should think of some new dialogue." Clement shrugged. "Maybe I am being unfair. Perhaps our dear Jane got lucky and was rolling the night away in an orgy of unrestrained passion. After all, we do have to do our research, don't we?"

I took a deep breath. The chill air in my lungs kept me from screaming. Snowed in with a bunch of kindergartners... What had I done to deserve this?

"Why don't I go up and see what's holding her?" I asked, and as soon as the words were out of my mouth I knew they were a mistake. That old ghost Grammy had told me about was stamping all over my grave. And in combat boots yet!

"I'll go with you." Ralph's grin was conspiratorial as his hand clamped onto my elbow once more. Drat it, he probably thought I volunteered just for the chance to be alone with him, the egotistical thing.

Surprisingly, it was Clement—a most unlikely white knight—who came to my aid. He took my other arm and made a flourishing gesture. "I hardly think that is necessary, Harcourt. If she goes with me, we'll all know she won't be...sidetracked. Not unless you've been keeping a big secret from everyone, dear Liz! Come along; let's go knock dear old Jane up…"

"Thank you for saving me," I said simply. I had waited until we were almost at the elevators before opening my mouth. Ralph Harcourt was a pest to have as a prospective suitor or editor, but I could imagine that he would be downright nasty as an enemy.

"My pleasure, dear girl. It's nice to know that there is one person whom we can both hate." He had released my elbow as soon as we were out of sight of the others. I don't think he liked any sort of physical contact with a woman. "Do you think that prolific cow is really going to leave Bernie?"

So I wasn't the only one who had a suspicious mind.

"Do you know where Jane's room is?"

"Right between you and me." He looked at me with surprise, one pale eyebrow arched sarcastically. "Vanessa is on the other side of you, and our dear Bernie and Anita are *en suite* on the other side of me. Don't you know our dear little Bernie likes to keep his little chicks under his thumb?"

"How do you know where everyone is?"

"Remember the cardinal rule, dear — research, research, research! I like to know who's sleeping next to me. Life is easier if you know who's where. And," he added salaciously, "who's doing who."

He was so ridiculous I couldn't help smiling. "If I didn't know you better, I'd swear..."

Clement looked pained. "Please don't, my dear girl. It's so undignified, you know."

* * *

The hallway was deserted except for a chambermaid's cart at the far end. There's always something slightly spooky about a long, windowless hotel corridor lined with closed doors. The symbolism is limitless, but I was more concerned with my claustrophobia. The only thing resembling a window was

66

a couple of panels of frosted glass in the elevator alcove not far from our group of rooms. It was not an area where I would want to spend any amount of time.

Jane's door was locked, and there was no answer to our knock. Clement continued to knock while I stepped into my room and tried to ring through on the telephone. Dimly, I could hear the ringing in the next room in sort of a ghostly counterpoint to the electronic buzz in my ear.

"No answer," I said needlessly, re-locking my door. "We must have passed her in the elevators, or she's out on some errand of her own. Let's go back down."

"Do you think she's down there?"

"Unless she's ill or something," Clement said sententiously. "It would be a pity to come all the way up here and..."

"All right, Clement Wallingford. Why do you want to get into her room?"

"What makes you think that I...?"

"Clement! Come off it! You want to see what she's working on, don't you?"

He squirmed. "Really, Liz... I...I just wanted to see if it's true that she has a band of enslaved dwarves who write all her books for her..."

I couldn't help it. I laughed. Clement could be maddening, but when he wanted, he could be very funny, too. I also knew that if he wanted to get into Jane's room to look around he would do it sooner or later. It might as well be while I was there to act as some sort of restraining influence.

"All right. Maybe the chambermaid can let us in."

It took some doing to convince the maid to unlock

the door, including our promise that she could come with us to make sure that nothing was disturbed, and that we were just checking to be sure our friend wasn't ill. I couldn't blame her; over the years hotel thieves must have used every story possible, and the staff was warned against all of them.

I'd like to say that at the last moment when her key was releasing the lock I had some sort of knowledge, some premonition of what was about to happen, but I didn't. Uppermost in my mind was the hope of getting this charade over quickly and getting back downstairs for another cup of hot coffee.

I didn't know that my life—all our lives—were about to be changed forever.

When the door opened all we could see was the end of the bed.

It was made up.

That did start a *frisson* along my spine, but it was one of near-excitement, not fear. The fear would come later. My thoughts then were more lighthearted; my room just next door had not yet been cleaned—had Jane found a boyfriend? Had she spent the night somewhere else? She must have; her bed was undisturbed, and I couldn't see even Jane Hall making up her own bed in a luxury hotel.

Then we saw where she had spent the night.

There was a shrill sound like a siren. I wondered how the police had gotten there so soon until I realized it was the maid screaming. That snapped me back to reality; if she hadn't screamed, I probably would have.

Clement turned to face me, his normally pale skin now definitely greenish. "Liz, I...I..." His eyes rolled upward, and he melted into a faint as gracefully as any of his heroines.

I couldn't spare him a thought. Inwardly and outwardly, I was frozen. Most of all, I most sincerely regretted having eaten that Danish.

Jane was sprawled in the narrow space between the bed and the wall, her basic black dress now blotted with rusty brown that, when fresh, had been bright red. Her eyes open but now dry looking, stared sightlessly at the ceiling.

She had been dead for a long time.

* * *

The next few hours were the worst I had ever lived through. Somehow we got the manager up there, and he got us out, locking the door behind him. Then we were all herded into his office while he called the Royal Canadian Mounted Police station down on the Banff highway. Even though it was only a few miles away down the mountain, I didn't see how they could possibly get through, but they did—barely.

An hour later, a long hour later, they came in stamping the snow off their boots, saying that their four-wheel drive had almost foundered and that the snow was falling more thickly than ever.

After a lifetime of devotion to Nelson Eddy in the old late night staple "Rose Marie", I was vaguely disappointed to see that they wore only simple brown uniforms with no fancy red coat in sight. Somehow that only added to the unreality of the situation.

All the time we had waited for them to come, I had been trying to convince myself that this truly was real, that it had really happened. It would have been easier to think that someone with a warped sense of humor had just played a sick kind of joke. I could easily have believed that Clement might be at the bottom of such a weird prank had he not been seated next to me, his greenish pallor only slightly lessened by the application of several brandies.

That and the fact that Jane was indubitably dead.

The maid, a local girl earning money for college, as was most of the staff, huddled in a corner and was being comforted by the assistant manager. She was still sobbing slightly.

Numb, I stared into space.

Until now the only dead people I had seen had been various elderly relatives called to the bosom of their Maker in the fullness of their time. They had lain in silken caskets, their wrinkled faces made up in a semblance of life, and everything had seemed so natural, so easy, so serene. They had passed away; they had not been murdered. Today I had seen death, death with none of the trimmings, death in all its ugly, raw nakedness for the first time, and I would never forget it.

"Miss Allison..." The Mountie repeated, touching my arm gently.

We had been moved up to an empty suite on the third floor that the Mounties were turning into a command post. Extra chairs had been brought in, as well as steaming pots of coffee. Someone had put a cup into my hands. It burned my fingers, but I clutched the pain as a symbol of my being alive.

Maybe I should have let Kevin come along, and then

I wouldn't feel so terribly alone. Of course, he would have taken the invitation to join me as another way of saying "yes" to his continual proposal, and as distressed as I felt, I still didn't know if I wanted to do that. One should be cautious and rational when considering marriage, but shouldn't there be something else? Something...

"Elizabeth, dear..." Anita said softly.

In the last few hours Anita Wingate had become a leaning post for all of us, showing strength and compassion none of us had ever thought she possessed. She moved her chair closer to mine and laid a comforting hand on my arm. Bernie, white-faced with shock, stared sightlessly out the window at the swirling white sky. Clement and the maid were being ushered into the outer room.

"I'm sorry, Sergeant Hunter. I...I'm all sort of scattered. My name isn't Allison..."

He looked interested at that, like a hound which has found an intriguing scent. Poor man, he dealt with a real-life world of concrete facts, not with make-believe as we did. I felt sorry for him once he tried to question Clement.

"It's my pen name...the name under which I write...under which I write romances. My real name is Elizabeth MacAllister."

He noted it on his pad. Sergeant Hunter really seemed to be a very nice man; average looking, average voice...he added a much needed note of normalcy to the macabre proceedings.

"Now, Miss—Miss?—MacAllister, what were the circumstances that led you to discover the body?"

How frivolous it all seemed now. Repeating Clement's comment about the dwarves, I felt as if I were saying something profane or obscene. The sergeant said nothing, but his disbelief was palpable.

"If you cannot find someone, do you always make it a practice to enter their hotel room?"

"No. We just wanted to see if she were there, if she were ill...or something. Jane is usually so punctual, so precise..."

"Were you and Miss Hall friends?"

"No. I really didn't care for her."

"Then how were you so aware of her habits?"

"Don't badger the poor girl!" Anita snapped, but the Mountie dismissed her with a wave of his hand.

"Anyone who knew Jane at all was aware of her habits. She is..." I caught my breath with a sob. "She was one of the most predictable people I ever met."

"That is true."

"Please, Mrs. Wingate..."

"You do want to know the truth, don't you?"

"Every six weeks," Bernie rumbled sonorously from the window.

"What?"

"Every six weeks. She could turn out a novel every six weeks, just like clockwork. I've got my printing schedule set up on that basis for the next year." He sounded stricken.

"Miss Hall was one of your better writers, then," Sergeant Hunter asked and was rewarded with a glare from Bernie. "I—I'm not familiar with the name."

"Jane Hall never used her own name..." Anita began

helpfully, but Bernie began to list her pseudonyms solemnly, as if intoning a roll call of the dead.

"Pauline Marshall, Marsha Paulson, LaWanda Tate, Clarissa Heatherington, Heather Clairmont, Annalise Bernard...that was the one she used for the first book she published with us. In honor of me..."

The Mountie looked rather stunned. "All those names?"

"Jane had at least fifteen names," Anita said primly. "I don't know if even she remembered them all. I'm sure if you contact her agent, she'll be able to get you a list..."

"In that case, I wonder who the killer was killing," he said slowly. "Miss Hall or one of her alter egos..." Poor man. He looked out of his depth. "Did Miss Hall have any jewelry?"

Anita shook her head. "I've never seen her wear anything of note."

"She had on a pin last night," I said. "It was a funny, old-fashioned bar pin...filigree, I think."

"We found that on her body," Sergeant Hunter said, consulting his notes. "As well as a small gold pinkie ring and a gold neck chain."

"Poor Jane, she never did have much of a sense of style," mourned Anita. "She could have afforded the crown jewels, but she seldom wore anything."

"Her purse was undisturbed, so I think we can rule out robbery. My partner is making an inventory of the place now, but I don't think we'll find anything missing."

Bernie turned in from the window. His face was ghastly. "I thought you couldn't disturb a crime scene."

"We do what we can. We've taken photographs of

everything." The Mountie cleared his throat; he was obviously uncomfortable. "I mean, we couldn't just leave the poor woman lying there..."

There was a small sound of pain, as if from a wounded animal, and I realized I was making it. I had never liked Jane Hall, but I couldn't think of anyone I disliked enough to wish such a fate.

"Please!" Anita hissed, her grip on my arm tightening. "Elizabeth is a very sensitive girl."

"I'm all right, really I am. What...what killed her? There was so much blood..."

"A knife. One of the hotel knives."

"That means it had to be one of the staff, doesn't it?" I asked, grasping at straws. Anything to distance this horrible crime from people like me. "I mean, to have had access to the kitchen knives..."

"No, ma'am. It was a regular table knife."

"You mean..." Anita's voice went tight with horror. She raised a dainty handkerchief to her mouth. "One like we eat with?"

The sergeant nodded. "A wooden handled steak knife. We've got it bagged, but I doubt there'll be any prints on it. There must be at least a thousand like it here in the hotel. There's even a set-up chest full of them just outside the Empress dining room."

Now Anita was clinging to me as much to be comforted as to comfort. "But we used some like that just last night."

I thought I might be sick. A lot has been written about how most of a queasy stomach is all in the mind, and now I believe it. One moment all I could think of was getting to a bathroom where I could throw up in peace, and the next, I had forgotten all about it.

We were all startled when the door flew open with a crash. Even the steadfast Sergeant Hunter jumped.

"Elizabeth!"

It was Jared, a wild-eyed, distraught Jared I had never seen before. In the comparative warmth of the room the snow was melting off his flapping parka and dripping like tears onto the carpet.

My response was instinctual and immediate. Without a word he held out his arms to me, and all thoughts of my queasy stomach forgotten, I flew into them, burrowing against him as I had so many other, happier times. My head still just fit in the hollow of his neck. His arms closed around me, wrapping me inside the parka with him. The warmth of him seemed to melt something deep within me, and the tears I had held back for so long began to ooze from under my eyelids.

"Elizabeth!" Anita's shocked voice was like a cold shower. Next to it Sergeant Hunter's growling, "Jerry, what the hell is this?" carried no weight at all.

We ignored them. Jared cradled me close, and our bodies fit together as if the bitter years had never been.

"I heard that one of the Wingate writers had been killed...a woman...I had to know it wasn't you," he crooned, one hand doing a slow circle in the middle of my back. He hadn't forgotten how much I loved that. His lips pressed against my hair. "I had to know you were all right."

"It was Jane Hall. I found her. Oh, Jared, she was right next door to me. While I was sleeping she was dead like that..." I began to shake again, and he held me even closer.

"You couldn't help that. Just so you're all right..."

"Jerry!" This time everyone heard the sergeant. "What is going on?"

"I had to make sure Miss MacAllister was all right."

"I was not aware you knew any of the staff here," Anita said repressively. "Elizabeth, who is this?"

Jared and I looked at each other. Even after all this time we could still sense each other's thoughts. Somehow he had managed to skin out of his parka without ever letting go of me. He tossed it into the corner while the ever-helpful Sergeant Hunter answered Anita's question.

"He's Jerry Grant. He plays piano in the lobby bar."

I looked up, and Jared gave me a crooked smile. There was nothing to be lost by telling the truth.

"Not really. I've just been going by the name of Jerry Grant."

"It's not your real name?" Sergeant Hunter's eyes bulged.

"No. My real name is Jared Granville."

"The concert pianist?" Now it was Anita's turn to be startled.

"Yes. And," I said, burrowing my head into his chest to avoid her penetrating gaze, "he's also my ex-husband."

* * *

That caused as much of an uproar as anything could, so much so that any further questions simply got lost in the babble. Finally, Sergeant Hunter threw up his hands in desperation.

"Quiet. *Quiet*! Jerry...Jared...whatever your name is...Do you know anything about this case?"

"No. I just wanted to be sure Elizabeth was safe." His arm tightened around my waist. It felt unbelievably reassuring. "Are you through with her for now, Pete?"

The Mountie nodded wearily. "Go ahead, get out of here. Just don't try to leave."

"In the middle of a blizzard? Come on, Pete." Jared scooped up his parka and shoved me out the door.

"Jared? Are you sure we should do this? I don't want you to get in trouble..."

"Really, Elizabeth, didn't you hear what I told Pete? There's a full-fledged blizzard going on out there. I barely made it down from Hillside House."

My body shivered with a cold that had nothing to do with the snow. "That means we're really trapped in here...with a murderer."

"Yes," he said gravely, then grabbed my shoulders with a painful earnestness. "But nothing is going to happen to you, understand? Nothing! You are going to be all right...I promise."

"Jared, I'm afraid. I've never been involved with anything like this..." I sounded like a whimpering little girl, and I didn't like it. "I want to get out of here."

He pushed the elevator button savagely, and then smiled at me with a gentleness I hadn't seen in a long time. "Elizabeth, I hate to keep reminding you, but there's a blizzard going on outside."

"I don't care! I feel like this place is closing in on me...I can't breathe..."

"Claustrophobic in a 375 room hotel?" he chuckled.

"Heaven help you if you ever have to spend a winter up here. Come on, we'll get your jacket. I think the covered walk to the annex is still passable. At least it'll get you outside for a few minutes."

The elevator girl gaped as we got in, arm in arm; I could just imagine the gossip that would flow among the employees after this.

"Where's your room?"

The elevator girl gasped.

"Second floor."

She almost missed it, and I could feel her eyes boring into us as we left. Either Jared was completely immune to the fluttering he set off in the hearts of the female employees, or he was so used to them he didn't care. Considering my experience with him, probably the latter...except for one. One very important one. Women had always worshipped him.

The door to Jane's room was closed. My hands began to shake so badly that Jared took the key and opened the door himself.

"She's not in there anymore," he said. "It's just an empty room, nothing more. Get your jacket."

I fumbled in the closet while Jared opened and closed the door, seemingly intent on breaking it down. It was a minute before I realized what he was doing.

"It seems a sound enough lock," he said at last, "but I want you to put the chain on just as soon as you come in, and don't open the door to anyone. Anyone!"

"Jared..." My lips were stiff. I couldn't really make them work correctly. "Do you think that...that he might want to kill me?"

"I've frightened you. I didn't mean to, Lillybet," he said softly, and neither one of us noticed that he used my old pet name. "I just want to be sure you're protecting yourself. I don't want you taking chances."

"Don't worry, I won't. And just as soon as I can get through all that dratted snow I'm getting out of here." I jerked up the zipper on my jacket.

"You're getting out of here now," he said with a sardonic smile. "And you won't like it."

* * *

He was right.

The lobby was fairly warm, due mainly to the milling press of people, but once we stepped outside, the cold snow hit us like an icily wet towel in the face. The annex was a smaller building done in pseudo-Tudor half-timbering, connected to the hotel proper by a roofed walkway. On the walkway itself the snow was barely ankle deep; apparently even the meager protection of the roof was helpful, for the rest of the world had vanished under a blanket of white. Every marker was lost. The lake, the rocks, the paths, even the snowman, all gone. Not even the short time we had lived in New York could have prepared me for such viciousness. It was as if Nature wanted to obliterate everything.

"Hardly," Jared said in answer to my comment. "It's her way of cleaning house... Starting fresh."

I let him know what I thought of that theory with a single, telling glance and then pointed to the annex. "What's there?"

"A restaurant, a club, some shops...It's only open in the summertime, I think."

Janis Susan May

We turned around and walked back to the hotel. Now the wind was in our face and, roof or no roof, the snow tore at our skin like a thousand tiny fingernails. It hurt to breathe. Why in the world would anybody choose to live in such a climate?

I glanced at Jared. In a way it was strange our being here like this, thrown once again into an atmosphere of intimacy. The cocooning snow surrounded us as if we were the only people in the world. I never would have said a word under any other circumstances; it was almost as if the storm blew it out of me.

"I'm sorry about Jennifer."

If he were startled I couldn't tell. "Thank you. That's nice of you to say."

Blast the man! Was that all he was going to say? I wanted to scream, to beat on him, to make him tell why he had left me for her. Was she prettier than I? Kinder? Better in bed? What did she have that I didn't? What had pulled him from my side to hers? What had I lacked?

Instead I said, "I heard you were hurt."

"I had some burns on my legs. They're all right now."

His voice was lifeless. I could only imagine the pain of living through a dreadful auto accident with only a few burns on your legs when the woman you loved died a horrible death.

We turned and walked back toward the annex. Now the wind was at our back again, and we could get our breath. The wind screamed around the corner of the hotel like a living thing seeking prey.

"We were breaking up, you know," he said

suddenly.

I stopped dead in my tracks. "No. I hadn't heard..."

"She said that music would always come first with me, and she couldn't bear being second. Come on, if you don't walk, you'll freeze to death out here."

I forced my legs to move. The words came tumbling out of their own volition. "Then how come you're playing junk music here?"

At first I didn't think he heard. We walked on through the deepening snow, reached the annex and turned back into the biting teeth of the wind.

"Because I've lost it, Elizabeth." His words were barely audible over the screaming snow. "I can't do it any more. I play the notes, and they come out garbage! I love and respect music too much to insult it."

I tried to think of something to say, of some way to comfort that awful gaping wound he had just exposed, but the words wouldn't come.

"I'm cold. Let's go in."

The lobby was more crowded now and the babble of conversation carried an edge of panic. The manager, looking very harassed, stood on one of the oak tables.

"I assure you that all precautions are being taken and that there is nothing to worry about! If we all work together everything will be all right. Road crews will be out as soon as the blizzard calms down, and until then, we have plenty of supplies. Mrs. Wilcox has set up an office in room 225 for those of you who are with the 'Just Write for Love' Conference. If you have questions about the conference, please see her. For the rest of you, the desk staff has been briefed, and I shall be in my office."

"Good grief," Jared breathed. "Poor Finlay will be mobbed. I better go see if I can help him. Will you be all right?"

I nodded. "Thank you, Jared...for everything. I think I'll go upstairs..."

"Be sure and put the chain on your door."

"I will," I said, but he didn't hear; he was already pushing his way through the crowd towards the office.

"Mrs. Granville?"

It had been so long since I had heard that name I didn't react for a moment. Then the officer asked again, this time lightly touching my arm.

"Excuse me, Mrs. Granville; may I have a few words with you? I'm Walters of the RCMP." He was a younger man than Hunter, but not as good looking.

"I'm sorry. I haven't used that name since the divorce. I...I didn't recognize... My name is MacAllister."

"Let's go in here." The lobby bar was still closed, though only a velvet rope barred the entrance. He unhooked it and then refastened it behind us. "I don't mind saying it gave us a bit of a turn to find out that old Jerry wasn't old Jerry after all and that he had a wife to boot."

I sat next to the big window. In more clement weather this would be the best view of the lake. Now, though, there might have been a curtain of white velvet hung outside the glass. The storm appeared to be thickening instead of abating.

And night would come, and there was a murderer loose...

"Ex-wife," I said automatically. "We were divorced two and a half years ago."

"Do you know why Jerry used a different name?"

That would seem to be Jared's story, but I was past such niceties. The vision of Jane Hall's bloody body haunted me.

"At one time he was a concert pianist. A Chopin specialist. There was an auto wreck in which a young woman died. He was not badly hurt. There was a great deal of bad publicity...Sometimes all fame is not to be desired."

He nodded slowly. "Yes, that tallies with what Mr. Finlay told us."

"The manager knew?"

"Yes. Apparently Jerry told him when he applied for the job."

Strange. I hadn't expected such integrity from Jared. Before, everything had been sacrificed to his music. Apparently, now his conscience demanded the sacrifice of both his music and his pride.

"Jerry's a good chap. Came and played for us at our big dinner-dance not long ago. Wouldn't take a penny, either..." Officer Walters shook his head. "Anyway, now that's all cleared up, there are a few questions I'd like to ask you."

"I've already talked to Sergeant Hunter..."

"I know, Miss MacAllister. He asked me to check these few points with you...First of all, when did you last see Miss Hall?"

"At dinner last night."

"Did you go upstairs together?"

"No, I went first. Jane and Bernie were talking business."

"So you didn't come down again until this morning."

"No, I stayed up there for a while then I got restless and decided to go for a walk."

"In the snow?"

"Last night I thought it was a novelty. We don't get much snow in Louisiana."

"Then?"

I told him of the meeting with Jared on the walk. It was pretty obvious that he didn't believe it was accidental. That was all right, since I wasn't too sure it had been, not really. Since coming here I hadn't been able to think too clearly. Had I wanted to see Jared when I left my room last night? Even I didn't know for sure.

"So you went to your room right after dinner, stayed there until after midnight and returned there before one a.m.?"

"That's about right, I guess. I didn't really watch the clock."

"Do you know of anyone who would want to kill Miss Hall?"

I shrugged. "I don't know of anyone who knew her well enough to want to kill her. She wasn't much of an individual...she never got close to anyone or responded to anyone...no one that I knew of, anyway."

"Sort of a cold fish."

Once again the vision of her, stiff and cold and splashed with her own blood, flashed into my mind. "I wish you hadn't said that, but I know what you meant.

84

Jane was a difficult woman to know. I don't know anyone who did."

"Mr. Wingate said that Miss Hall had been stalked by a fan some years ago. Do you know anything about that?"

It was one of the few things about Jane Hall that was public knowledge. A fan, one of the few who knew of Jane's many pseudonyms, became convinced that she was Jane Hall's lover. She had bombarded Wingate Publications, the book distributor and all the Wingate authors with letters pleading for their intercession in their 'lover's quarrel'. Then she had somehow gotten Jane's personal address; I always thought Clement the villain there. Jane was infuriated; she actually went on several chat shows to expose her tormentor as a former mental patient with a history of stalking. She had made mincemeat of the woman, using her gift for words and not inconsiderable resources without restraint until the stalker had been locked in the back of some distant mental hospital and the key ostensibly lost. When asked why she had been so vehement, Jane had replied that she disliked being harassed, and she disliked being insulted; then she had vanished back into the privateness of her own life.

"Only what was common knowledge. I wasn't a Wingate writer at the time. Do you think that woman has gotten loose?"

"We're checking on that," he replied abruptly.

"Tell me...do you really regard me as a suspect?"

The young Mountie looked down at his papers. His face was blank. "Right now, Miss MacAllister, everyone is a suspect."

"Including me."

"Including you."

Chapter Five

I hadn't really planned on going to a party, but after a couple of hours alone in my room—with the door double locked and chained—I was so jittery and sick of my own company that almost anything else was preferable. Not having planned for much leisure I hadn't brought anything to read, and the two manuscript notebooks, one now empty, mocked me from the desk, making the idea of working on either *Daughters* or *Man* out of the question.

Twice a woman had knocked on the door, each time claiming to be a reporter, but I had just sat still and quiet, and eventually she had gone away. Before we found Jane, Bernie had been complaining that most of the media had been content to do their reporting from nothing more than airport interviews; that's why the press conference I had been so careful to miss had been held in Banff. He had lamented that there were no reporters left here to cover the conference.

If he had known there would be no media presence here, would Bernie have announced the change to Wingate Romances at the press conference in Banff? Or had he banked that they would be here for the conference itself, and then the blizzard fouled everything up?

There was one reporter, admittedly, but she seemed to be as persistent as the worst of them. I had never had a very high opinion of the entire breed even before they had hounded me for days after Jared's accident. I hadn't had anything to say then, and I didn't have anything to say — for public consumption — now.

Another thought. Surely Bernie wouldn't....? He was a ruthless businessman, certainly, but he wouldn't, he couldn't use poor Jane's death as a publicity ploy...

Of course he would.

Winifred MacDougal had been right when she called Bernie ruthless. If it would save Wingate Publications...Wingate *Romances*, he would use anything that came to hand.

What if the rumors were true that Jane had been thinking about leaving him? In spite of all the business about the 'Fabulous Four' and Wingate's other romance writers, it was Jane's prodigious output that was the company's bread and butter. Her departure to another house would...

That line of thought was too ridiculous to pursue. I couldn't think of it now.

I couldn't think of anything but how I had slept here last night, while just beyond that thin wall of lath and plaster lay...

If I could only have gotten out... I stalked the tiny room, back and forth, back and forth...It was an unsatisfying exercise. At home I was outdoors half the time, winter and summer. I paced the tiny room and tried to convince myself the walls really weren't closing in on me. Funny, I had never felt this trapped in New York, but then I had had reason to be happy staying indoors...

No use thinking along that line. Jared might seem different, but it was foolish to think that he had changed fundamentally. After a while he would get over his wash of guilt and be the same egocentric, selfish creature he had always been. He had had extreme moods before; I had been lucky to get out before this one set in.

If I repeated that often enough I might start to believe it.

Blast this snow! I would have braved even the company of a murderer just for a walk along the lake. Of course, that was a fairly empty boast. Outside, the snow still fell steadily, and it was impossible to see even where the lake had been under that fluffy white blanket. Jared had laughed about my being claustrophobic in a 375 room hotel, but it was no laughing matter. I was beginning to go slightly bonkers.

Which is how I ended up at tea with Anita and Bernie. I hadn't particularly wanted so see anyone, but when I had finally decided to go downstairs I couldn't say no when they beckoned me over to their table. Besides that, I was starving.

Anita, this afternoon wearing a devastating little green wool dress, cast a disparaging glance at my slacks, but it was a sign of her mood that she said nothing. Today almost everyone in the place was dressed more for warmth than for style; the results were a great deal more harmonious than yesterday's fashion show had been.

The tea area was crowded, but somehow there were two empty tables flanking the Wingates'. Apparently everyone thought murder might be catching. As I walked across the lobby in response to Bernie's wave, the babble of conversation faltered and died then swelled again behind me. I could feel every eye in the place following me like dirty little fingerprints.

If this were what being a celebrity was all about, I didn't like it at all.

"Grim, isn't it?" Bernie motioned to the waitress, and a place setting materialized for me. "The same thing happened to us."

"Vulgarians!" Anita muttered with a sniff. Only her papery-white fingers, strangling a wrinkled handkerchief, showed she was under any strain.

"Agreed." I poured a cup of tea, thinking too late that perhaps I had stopped too soon. Maybe it would have been better to have kept on going into the bar and order a stiff drink. "Probably this is the most exciting thing that's happened in all their lives."

"Easy for them."

"Who would want to kill Jane?" Bernie asked of no one in particular. He looked pathetic, ashen-faced and blank. In the last few hours he had aged ten years. If it had been any other female besides Jane Hall, I might have wondered if they had had something going. With Jane the idea was ludicrous, and that in itself was sad.

"I can't imagine. Did she have any family?"

"None that any of us knew about. The Mounties are trying to get hold of Joyce Williams. She'd know if there were anyone or not."

I bit thoughtfully into a sandwich without really tasting it. How heartbreaking that Jane and Bernie had worked so closely for so long and yet they had to call her agent to see if she had any family.

"That's terrible," I said slowly. "She's given so much pleasure to so many, and no one seems to know anything about her."

"She wasn't an easy person to know," Anita said, interweaving her fingers through the tortured handkerchief.

"Every six weeks. A new book every six weeks."

"Oh, for Heaven's sake, Bernard!"

"I wonder if that's why she was murdered." I murmured. I had heard horror tales of other conventions, where authors had been stalked by demented fans or would-be writers, either for some sort of ego gratification or determination that they had some magic secret to getting published. Jane had been stalked once. What if that deranged woman were here, sitting calmly drinking tea a few tables away...?

I could have screamed.

The babble behind us swooped and rose again, announcing another visitor. None of us were very pleased to see that it was Clement, but there was nothing Anita could do except to ask him to sit down.

"Ah, my fellow pariahs! I see you too are being given a most unmetaphoric cold shoulder. Tea...An inhuman drink, but at least warming." He motioned to the waitress for utensils and then poured himself a cup with theatrical grace. "And what are you all discussing on this cold and wretched day? How foolish of me to ask...dear Jane, of course. I always said she would do anything to sell a few extra copies."

"Oh, really!" Anita snorted in disgust.

"Clement, that's no way to talk about poor Jane." I snapped.

"Poor Jane. Amazing how the most loathsome

person acquires immediate canonization by the simple act of dying. Don't glare at me like that, dear Liz! While she was breathing no one ever thought of saying 'poor Jane' in such charitable tones, but now that she has been snuffed..."

Anita's handkerchief ripped. "Really, Clement! You are utterly despicable."

"I don't know what we're going to do," Bernie said morosely. He didn't seem to have heard any of the wrangling. I began to wonder if he and Jane actually had had something going.

"What are you talking about, Bernie?" I asked.

"Wingate Romances. I've already sent out the press releases and set up the publishing schedules..."

"Without even mentioning it to me? You notified the press before you told me?" an aghast Anita cried, but her husband ignored her.

"...and without Jane...I had counted on her."

"And you never told me..." Anita said in a hard, tight voice.

"Does this mean you'll have to change... everything?"

"I hope not, Liz. It would mean a great deal of revenue lost if I did. I've already signed a very large distribution contract. The distributors would never forgive me."

I could believe that. A publisher who promised and then didn't deliver was quickly relegated to the back shelves, particularly if a big publicity campaign was involved. Knowing Bernie, the puffery for Wingate Romances would be only slightly less than for the Second

Coming.

Anita took a deep breath and laid a comforting hand on her husband's arm. "I know it will be difficult, dear, but surely Wingate Publications will survive. There will always be a market for quality books...The distributors will understand, especially after poor Jane's death..."

"Had you depended so very much on Jane?" I asked.

Bernie nodded gloomily and Clement, his voice unadulterated acid, said, "Of course he did. She was Superwoman, didn't you know?"

"If you don't shut up..."

"You'll do what, dear Liz? Murder me?"

A strangled sob came out of Anita's tightly clenched mouth. "How can you joke about it, you dreadful man? It's horrible, horrible, I say. That woman is dead. She is dead, and I was probably the last person to see her alive! It could have been me who was killed! Me!" The handkerchief shredded into flakes under her hysterical fingers.

Ever the lady, Anita had not raised her voice, but even so it was startling to watch her control vanish. She was trembling and terribly white around the mouth as if she might faint at any moment. Brandy would have been better, but there wasn't any to hand, so I grabbed the teapot, filled her cup and held it out.

"Here, Anita. Drink this."

Bernie helped lift the cup, saucer and all, to his wife's shaking lips. Anita took it, drank a tiny sip, then another, and finally her shaking stopped.

"Thank you. May I have some milk, please?"

"Are you all right, Honey?" Bernie slopped a dollop

of milk into her cup. A drop splashed onto the saucer, and she frowned.

"Just what happened, Anita? I didn't realize..." I said, willing Clement to be quiet with a hard glance. There wasn't anything to worry about there, not really; Clement hated any scenes he didn't create himself.

"Yes, Honey, tell us...You didn't mention anything about this earlier." It was a sign of Bernie's concern that he spoke so tenderly to his wife. He worshipped her, but they were not normally a demonstrative couple. In fact, they were an oddly mismatched pair, Anita, so beautifully cool and patrician despite her slum origins, and blue-blooded Bernie (back to the Mayflower on his mother's side) who had the appearance and disposition of a genial truck driver.

Anita nodded. "It was after most everyone had gone upstairs. Jane and Bernard and I were having a drink in the bar...Jane was so interested in the new project...."

"Yes, she was," Bernie agreed mournfully.

"Then she decided to go upstairs." Anita fished in her tiny bag for a fresh handkerchief. "I was tired, so I thought I'd go up with her. Bernard wasn't ready to come up yet..."

"Madelyn Edmonds was at the next table." He said it simply, with no apology and both Clement and I understood. Business was business.

Madelyn Edmonds was Peters and Worcester's top romance writer, and Jane Hall's only real competition. A lanky woman who looked like she would be more at home on the range than creating elegant scenes of historic passion, Madelyn was a writer of prodigious output and consistent quality; Bernie would never give up a chance to bring her over to Wingate Romances.

"Anyway, it wasn't until we were in the elevator that I realized I didn't have a key. I rode up with Jane, then back down to get the key from Bernard. Once I got back to the bar I got involved talking with Bernard and Miss Edmonds, and it was close to an hour before we finally went back upstairs."

"How horrible!" I said with feeling. It must be dreadful to know that only the chance of not having a key had kept her from being upstairs while a horrible murder had been committed.

It was worse to know that the murder had probably occurred while I had been in bed just next door, futilely trying to sleep.

Something vaguely important danced lightly through my mind, only to vanish at Anita's next words.

"And that isn't the worst thing," Anita went on in a tight little voice. "I think I saw her murderer."

She couldn't have had more of our attention if she had stood up and screamed. Even Clement had dropped his pose of *ennui* and was sitting forward in suspense.

"Well?" he asked. He was so interested he forgot to drawl. That was a first.

"Just before the elevator door closed I saw someone..."

"Could you tell who he was?" I asked.

"No, I guess I should, but I didn't see that much..."

Bernie had put a protective arm around her shoulders. "Tell us what you saw, Honey."

"Like I said, it was just a quick glimpse...I barely saw

anything, just that it was a man, and he was tall...tall and pale..."

"Bitch!" Clement's cup crashed on the floor as he jumped to his feet. Every eye in the place was now on us for sure. "You're trying to incriminate me. Everyone knows my room is next to Jane's...You've never liked me, never... Damned stuck-up..." Then he began swearing, calling Anita names that should never be put into print.

I yanked on his jacket, pulling hard enough to jerk him back down into his seat. "Shut up, you idiot!"

"But she..."

"Anita didn't mean anything by it. You are not the only tall, pale man in the hotel." I babbled on in a hoarse whisper, saying the first thing that came into my head.

All around the lobby every face was turned towards us, expressions ranging from distaste to avidity. It was extremely unpleasant.

"I know we weren't that fond of Jane, but is this any way to treat anyone's memory?" I went on desperately. "Besides, everyone is staring."

Still sulking, he leaned back. There was something ugly in his eyes, like a cornered rodent.

"Well, isn't this fortunate!" Her voice just oozing sugary insincerity, a young woman dressed in a flashy ski outfit walked right up to the table. "Almost all of the Wingate group together.... I've been trying to talk to you all...Taylor Huggins, from Multinational News Service..."

I knew a stringer when I saw one, even when she looked like the model for a 'Barbie™ Goes Skiing' doll. By now we all knew she was an aspirant writer, perhaps even a conference attendee who just by being here during the blizzard had fallen into a pot of butter, career-wise.

"Please go away," Bernie said with dignity barely covering his anger. "I have told you we have nothing to say to you."

She smiled, showing an extremely large number of very white teeth, sort of like a wolf. "But you're saying it to everyone, shouting like that. Now to get your story told..."

"We don't want to talk to you," Bernie repeated, this time with less dignity.

She smiled blindingly at the rest of us. "Surely you want to make sure you're correctly quoted...This is a tremendous story."

"And you are a vulture," I snapped, remembering the reporters who had hounded me for a quote after Jared's accident. "Now go away."

"Tragedy seems to follow you, doesn't it, Miss MacAllister?" Taylor looked around for a chair, but there was none within easy reach. "That poor woman killed when your former husband..."

"Which has nothing to do with anything here," I spat the words at her like poison darts and almost wishing they were. Jared didn't deserve to have all that raked up again. Maybe she wouldn't find out about him...

"Miss Huggins..." said Bernard in reasonable tones.

"And everyone knows what trouble Mr. Wallingford has had with the press, though I wonder how many of his fans realize that's his real name..."

Clement looked up; if he weren't a murderer (and I seriously doubted that he was) he certainly seemed as if he could become one quite quickly. He called Miss

Huggins something short, sharp and thoroughly unprintable.

"That's just what I mean...Is that the kind of press you want to have?" She smiled brightly. "Now, I'm a writer too, and I know what kinds of pressures face us...I'm the only representative of the press here, and I want to be sure that you're treated fairly..."

"That sounds a great deal like blackmail, Miss Huggins."

Her smile faded into something ugly as she turned to Anita. "That's a *passé* word, Mrs. Wingate, and an unfair one. I'm just saying that there are two ways of saying the same thing, one unflattering and one flattering. I want..."

"There is only one way of saying the truth," Anita said in a clear, bright voice that carried, "no matter what you threaten. We have nothing to fear from the truth."

Now, tangible as a breeze, everyone's gaze swept to Taylor Huggins. She flushed an unflattering red. "You're being very foolish, Mrs. Wingate. I just want to get a story..."

"And we just want for you to leave us alone," Bernard said in a voice that matched his wife's. "I intend to call Helmut Hoffman, head of MNNS, and tell him what his hirelings are up to. And—if you really are a MNNS rep, which I question—you should know the difference between reporting the news and slanting the news. Now, will you leave us alone, or shall I have one of the Mounties make sure that you do?"

"I won't forget this," she hissed, but it was a weak threat, with no real power behind it. So stiff her hands were clenched into fists at her side, she turned and stalked away.

"Bravo!" I whispered to Bernie.

"Well done, old man!" added Clement in a tone I had never heard from him.

"I'm afraid that's going to cost me unless I start doing some damage control right now," Bernie said, the lines between his brows deepening to chasms. "I've got to call our publicity department, and I'd better talk to some of the big news guns personally..."

"I didn't say it was you, Clement," Anita said suddenly in a small voice. It was almost lost in the sudden babble that rose to fill the enormous silence.

"Have you told this to the Mounties?"

Anita favored me with a withering look. "Of course. They even confirmed it with the elevator girl."

"So that's why they asked me when you came back to the bar." Bernie said suddenly. "I thought they were checking my alibi."

Braver than the rest, one waitress dashed in, picked up Clement's shattered cup and left him a fresh one. She did not, however, stay to pour. I had to do that.

"And I'm still a suspect," Clement growled, taking the cup without a thank you.

"Clement, until the murderer is found, we're all suspects. Officer Walters told me so. Even me, and I'm certainly not a tall, pale man."

"Elizabeth, not really!" Anita sounded truly shocked.

"Liz, the eternal peacemaker..." Clement was still growling, but his drawl was back, and he sounded more like himself. Metaphorically I heaved a sigh of relief, inwardly swearing that if I ever got out of this I would never come north of the Mason-Dixon Line again.

"Of course!" Bernie exclaimed. From a scowling man worrying about news coverage he had suddenly metamorphasized into a child on Christmas morning. The rest of us regarded him as we would an armed bomb.

"Of course what, Bernard?"

"I can kill two birds with one stone...It'll be great publicity."

Clement and I looked at each other in alarm.

"I've been wondering what to do about Wingate Romances...I can make the announcement when I call the newsboys..."

"What are you talking about, Bernie?" I asked hesitantly.

"We're going on with it. You two, Liz and Clement, and Vanessa, too, are going to have to take on the bulk of the writing...I'm going to have to ask you to double your schedules..."

"Bernard!" Anita breathed in distress, but Bernie, his eyes shining, ignored her. He scrabbled for pen and paper and began jotting down notes about production schedules.

"Double..." Clement and I breathed together, our alarm turning to dismay, and in my case, at least, pure panic. Neither of us had been exactly prolific in the last few months.

"Yes, double," Bernie chortled happily. "Maybe triple. I'm depending on you."

"Aren't you going to sign up some new writers?"

Pariah-dom only goes so far, and when aspirant novelists get wind of being published, it doesn't go very far at all. Once again a great deal of attention was focused on us, and a low undercurrent of excited conversation skittered around the room.

I felt like an actress on stage in some absurdist play. In a few minutes we would take our bows to hearty applause, the curtain would come down, and it would all be over.

No such luck. Like it or not, this was real life.

"Yes, but they will take time to develop."

"Darling, you're grasping at straws..." Anita laid a tender hand on her husband's sleeve. "Elizabeth and Clement are craftsmen; they can't be pushed like that. With things as they are now, Wingate Romances hasn't much of a chance. I'm sorry, dearest, but..."

"No, no, you don't understand. It just came to me...I've got the reprint rights to most of Jane's books; we'll do a special re-issue of them — one or two a month, in a special binding, with special bookmarks and maybe even a special case..." His eyes glowed with excitement.

"Are you serious, dear boy?"

"Yes. Can't you see it now? *'Wingate Romances presents a Memorial Edition to the Genius of Jane Hall.'*" Bernie's hand sketched the title in the air, as if he were already putting it on a special sale banner. "Of course, we'll have to have a big publicity campaign revealing all her names...I'll hint at that when I talk to the news boys this afternoon..."

Ghoulish as it was, it was a marketable idea. Probably it would sell books like crazy. I thought the concept nauseating, rather like dancing on a grave, except poor Jane didn't even have a grave yet.

Clement calmly nibbled at a *petit four*, but there was a tightness around his mouth. I wondered if he objected on moral grounds, or because even in death Jane got higher billing than he.

"Bernard, that is the most disgusting, disrespectful thing I have ever heard," Anita said in a low, hard voice.

"No, it's not disrespectful at all. Jane wanted her books to be read, and now that she can't write any more...it's the least we can do for her fans."

Clement gave a strangled, "Oh, really."

"Besides, she'd be the first to approve it," Bernie added.

There, he was quite right. Jane probably would—as long as she got a decent cut of the royalties.

A shiver ran down my spine. Who would benefit from Jane's death? My mind shied away from the obvious. Did she even have an heir, and was he/she/it here?

"Oh, shame on you. You're having a party and no one told me."

Our number was increased. Her voice perfectly modulated to be audible to the entire tea area without seeming to be overly loud, Vanessa flitted over to our table. She was the only woman I had ever met who could legitimately flit in a fur coat roughly the size of a bedspread.

Clement made a great show of procuring a chair and a place setting for her. The waitress, as goggle-eyed as the rest of the crowd, brought a fresh pot of tea and more sandwiches and sweets, a greater assortment than before. Vanessa had that sort of effect on people.

"I must tell all of you to be very careful...there is a most unpleasant young woman who was intent on talking to me about poor Jane...she made all kinds of vague threats about what would happen if I didn't cooperate."

"What did you do?" Bernard asked.

"I told her that I would be most happy to discuss my upcoming releases with her, or give her an interview about my new home fashions line, but I refused to talk about anything as tragic or tawdry as poor Jane's death. She became quite obscene."

Clement laughed. "Good girl. Stiff upper and all that."

Vanessa blinked. It was as kind a thing as he had ever said to her, perhaps the only kind thing.

"She was here, too," I said. "And I agree with you. She's a most unpleasant person."

"I don't think I have to caution all of you to be very careful of Taylor Huggins," Bernie said seriously. "She could be very damaging to Wingate Romances."

"Anyone out to build a reputation could be very dangerous," Clement said just too loudly. Considering that we sat in as dense a concentration of unpublished romantic novelists as one would be likely to find, it could have been taken as an insult.

"Really!" Anita snapped. Apparently the truce was over.

"Probably wants to solve the murder herself," Clement went on, but he did lower his voice. "What better way to get attention?"

"Do you really think so? I found her most unladylike, but so many young women are these days...It's this awful women's lib...If women just realized that the true path to happiness is being a wife and mother..." Vanessa trilled, just loud enough to be heard by most of the tea area.

"And ambition is certainly not ladylike," Clement replied sarcastically. "I tell you what, Bernie; you're looking for publicity for Wingate Romances...Why don't we solve the mystery of our tragically slaughtered comrade? Just imagine what a news story that would generate?"

I couldn't tell if he were kidding or not; sometimes with Clement it was difficult.

Anita didn't even try. She stood abruptly. "If you are going to talk such horrible rubbish, I am going upstairs. Bernard?"

Bernie stood automatically. He looked downcast that we hadn't been as enthusiastic about his great idea as he, but that wouldn't stop him. Once he got the bit in his teeth, he'd get what he wanted no matter what. As his pampered pets we seldom saw his tough side, but there were tales in the industry of his ruthlessness.

I suppose, had Jane died in a nice antiseptic hospital, of some socially acceptable illness, with all the proper rites and rituals, we would have found her death less shocking. It was illogical, perhaps, but the thought of re-issuing her books when she laid stiff and cold from an assassin's knife was repugnant.

"Of course," Bernie said. "I'll come with you."

Clement wasn't ready to give up; I guess he had been good just about as long as he could. "Are you two girls game, darlings? Shall we find out who killed Jane?"

"Clement," I said gently, "this is a romance writers' conference, not a mystery writers'."

"Don't be banal, dear Liz. One should never set limits on one's talent," he said more to Anita's retreating back than to either of us.

It was obvious that he meant it in a snide, nasty way, trying to get a rise out of Anita, but that trite phrase touched me in a way he had never intended. One should never set limits on one's talent. Hadn't that been what Anita was trying to tell me the day before? How odd that two such different people could say something and still say the same thing—though with two such opposite inflections.

Perhaps it was just a reaction to all the ugliness and upset surrounding Jane's murder, but suddenly it was as if a gate opened and sentences for *A Man of Honor* began to form in my mind. More than that, I knew that they would be easy to put down without problem or snarl.

"Lord, I hate that cold hearted bitch," Vanessa murmured in a barely audible whisper. This was no image she wished to share with her public.

Clement, too, was looking daggers at Anita. "This is an historic day. For once, dear Vanessa, we are in complete agreement."

"I don't understand you two. What have you got against Anita?"

"Of course you wouldn't, Liz; you are her darling. She has no use for any of the rest of us, in spite of the fact that it's our work that puts steak on her table and mink on her back. Besides," Vanessa answered tartly, "for someone of her background she certainly gives herself airs. I find her an insufferable snob."

"Miau, miau," Clement purred, now in his element. "I can't stand the bloody culture vulture either, but I guess it takes one to know one, my dear."

"What are you suggesting? That woman came up out of a slum."

"And a darn good job she did of it, too." I tried, but — glares locked like horns — they were too far-gone to hear the voice of reason.

A knowing grin slid over Clement's face like dirty oil, making it ugly. "And in what palace did you first see the light of day, Miss Goldberg?"

At the mention of her real name Vanessa flushed and bared her teeth for all the world like an angered animal. Very little was known about her early life, but one thing for sure was that it had not been spent in the rarefied social strata that was so lovingly described in her biography.

Suddenly, I felt dirty just sitting between the two old cats. Dear Heaven, if I could just get out of this place...Even staying in my room now seemed comparatively delightful.

The direction of attack changed. Vanessa's glittering eyes fastened on me, and like the passerby cornered by the venerable ancient mariner, I found myself unable to move.

"And you," she said silkily, "you are indeed the dark horse. Are the rumors I've been hearing about you and that absolutely darling piano player true?"

So much for any hope of keeping that particular story quiet. If Vanessa knew about it, then everyone would know about it, including that horrid hopeful reporter. I'd have to warn...I took a deep breath. Jared was not my responsibility any longer. He could hold his own with any reporter.

"Yes, dearest Liz..." Clement turned on me too. "It was too bad of you not to say anything when I was positively eating my heart out about him. Didn't anyone ever tell you it was naughty to keep secrets?"

I truly did want to scream.

Instead, I said as calmly as I could, "I don't know what rumors you've heard, but Jared...Jerry...is my ex-husband. I haven't seen him for years and didn't know he would be here until we ran into each other."

"And we never even knew you'd been married. You must tell us all about him." Vanessa leaned forward avidly.

"Yes, darling Liz, what other tasty secrets are lurking in your past?"

Vampires. Human vampires. Maybe by then I was getting a little hysterical, but they were going for the jugular. No, not for blood itself, but for something just as vital—emotions, real life feelings that they must simulate on paper but could never really feel themselves. The rest were just as bad, with their watching and staring and...I thought I just might be sick.

"Nothing to tell, really." I tossed off the question, popped one more *petit four* and stood up.

Apparently, not even murder and scandal were

enough to frighten away the unpublished. In a few minutes the surrounding tables would be converging on us. The signs were obvious; the furtive glances, the rummaging for pad and pen, the last minute preening. I was going to be out of there before that started.

"You're not leaving…"

"Of course I am, Vanessa…" Maliciously I raised my voice just a bit. "I know how much you look forward to your time alone with Clement…"

I was out and away beyond the ropes before they could close their mouths.

Chapter Six

He caught me at the elevators.

"Elizabeth!"

I did wish he hadn't been so public about it. Calling my name in front of the newsstand and then running half the length of the lobby was not the most subtle move in the world. The fact that he— sedate, arrogant, mannered darling of the upper crust—had done it at all was astonishing. It had been an afternoon of startling moments.

"Wait a minute!"

The elevator left without me. From beyond the velvet rope I could feel dozens of avid eyes devouring us.

Vampires!

"What's wrong, Jared?"

Up close he looked bad. There was a harried look about him, a strain that I had never seen before, even when he was working his hardest on mastering a new piece of music.

"You look terrible." I blurted involuntarily. "What have you been doing?"

"Helping Finlay out. The manager. The place has been a hotbox all day. Where are you going?"

"Back up to my room. I got bored up there, but it's getting a little thick down here."

A quicksilver grin split his face. "I'm not surprised. Who are that precious pair you were sitting with?"

"She's Vanessa Mangold. He's Clement Wallingford,

more often known as Aurora Wall and Jessica Fordham. They're two of Bernie's top writers."

"Part of 'The Fabulous Four', eh?"

I looked at him in surprise. "How did you know that?"

"Curiosity. I asked a few questions."

Strange. Curiosity had never been his strong point, especially about something not directly related to his music. Neither could I picture him wearing himself out doing a favor for a friend when he had to play that night. Of course, cocktail piano was nowhere near as demanding as concert work, but still...Curiouser and curiouser.

"You look tired."

"I am," he admitted. He smiled, but it was forced. "Finlay's been on the phone with the news media for hours, so I got the brunt of the guests. Damn bunch of hysterical females."

That last bitter line at least sounded more like the old Jared, though it had been most often applied to the gaggle of star-struck women who hung around his dressing room, hoping for a word or a glance from the great man. At first I had been a little jealous of those classical groupies, for there had been some very good-looking and wealthy women in the crowd, and Jared was a man who fed on adulation. Then, as his contempt for them had become obvious I had relaxed, secure that I was the only important woman in his life. I had quit worrying and devoted more time to the final drafts of *A Woman of Quality*.

When I looked up from that, I had found him

moving out of our apartment and into Jennifer's waiting arms.

I bit my lip savagely. That was all over and done with. Jennifer was dead, and Jared had been punished more than enough for his transgressions. It was just an accident that we had met again, and once this cursed snow melted I would be able to run south as fast as I could, back to civilization, back to...Kevin?

"What's wrong, Elizabeth?"

I had forgotten how sensitive he could be to another's moods. It had been one of his charms — when he chose to exercise it.

"Nothing. This is all just starting to get to me."

Behind us, the elevator opened with a whoosh.

"Come on," he said companionably and took my arm. "I'll take you to your room."

The elevator girl's eyes goggled.

"That's not necessary..."

"Come on." His fingers tightened on my arm in the old way, and I docilely preceded him into the spacious car.

During the early part of our marriage we, as do most couples, I suppose, had worked out a system of signals. We were nearly always touching in those days, and when someone asked a question or offered something or suggested a new diversion, we could communicate our real opinions by a touch. Whatever was said, if our fingers remained limp, the other could take it or leave it, but if the grip tightened, the other knew there was to be no arguing. It worked as well as any other system, I guess, except this time he was going to leave bruises on my elbow. Most people don't realize what strong hands pianists have, especially the pianists themselves.

We didn't say anything until the door of my room was safely closed behind us.

Very conscious of the elevator girl's stare, I had fished in my bag and handed the key to Jared. That was another old habit; Jared had always had a thing about locks. The girl was still staring when we closed the door. I could just imagine what my reputation was becoming.

It kept me from thinking about the yellow police tape stretched across Jane's door.

Once inside, Jared went through a thorough search, looking in the tub and closet, anywhere someone might hide, even under the bed. It should have made me feel secure, knowing that no one was there, but instead, his thinking that someone *might be* made me shiver.

"Did you really think there might be someone there?"

"No need to take any chances."

"Oh... Jared! I meant to tell you...there's this woman claiming to be a reporter..."

He scowled. "Taylor Huggins, Girl Reporter? I've already had the pleasure. Has she been bothering you?"

"She tried. Bernie sent her away, but I bet she'll be back."

"I can guarantee it."

"Sit down...You don't have to stand up like a tin soldier. Have you talked to the Mounties? Is there anything new?"

"Yes and no. They're still investigating, but without access to a lab there's not much they can do besides talk to people."

Without thinking I sat on the side of the bed and was relieved when he chose the desk chair. "Do they think there's going to be another murder?"

"They don't know. Do you?"

That was like being punched in the stomach. Could Jared really believe...?

"I? Why do you ask that? Surely you don't think I..."

"Of course not, silly. You could never kill anybody. If you could have, you would have killed me long ago."

"Probably."

He ignored me. "I asked that because you know these people. Is there anything you've noticed...?"

"That's just it. I don't really know these people. I knew Anita and Bernie, of course, and I had met Clement and Vanessa and...and Jane, but that's all."

"All?"

"When did you become a Mountie?" I asked crossly. "OK, by the book. I don't recall ever meeting any of the conferees before. As for the professionals, the writers and the agents and the editors, I guess I've met about half of them, but even that's been casually, at book conventions and authors' luncheons and that sort of thing."

"Any idea why Jane Hall?"

"No. I would have said that Jane Hall was the least likely person in the whole world to be murdered."

"Why?"

"She was such a nonentity that I don't think she could have inspired the passion necessary for such an act. I've thought about it, Jared, and if you'd asked me who might be a candidate for murder, I would have said

Clement or Vanessa more than Jane."

"But Jane Hall sold the most, didn't she?"

I eyed him narrowly. "You have been doing your homework, haven't you?"

He shrugged. "The Mounties told me. They came down to use the phone in Finlay's office. He has a direct line, so they didn't have to worry about someone listening through the switchboard. Not that it made much difference; the lines went down a little while ago."

"Down?" A shiver not connected to the frosty windows went over me with a blast of atavistic fear. "That means..."

"We've been isolated since the road was closed, but just as soon as the snow stops falling the Mounties will get some sort of a vehicle up here. This late in the season it can't be more than a day or two at most until things are back to normal..."

"A day or two!" I cried. He might as well have said one or two weeks. Jumping up, I started to pace.

"For Heaven's sake, Lillybet, settle down."

"Jared, do you think there are going to be any more murders?" There was a panicky note in my voice I didn't like.

The solid grip of his hands on my arms stopped both my pacing and my circulation. "I don't know, but until Jane Hall's murder is solved, you've got to be extra careful."

"I keep thinking of her, lying there dead, just next door...Jared, she's not still here, is she?" I looked quickly at the wall that separated my room from the death chamber, almost as if expecting to see Jane's poor limp body propped up against it.

"No, of course not. They took her down to one of the cold storage rooms downstairs. It's just a room, Lillybet. There's nothing in it. It shouldn't frighten you."

That was easy for him to say. He didn't have to sleep next to it.

"I don't want to stay here, Jared. I know I won't get a wink of sleep, not with that next door, even if it is empty. I'm going to change rooms..."

He released my arms as if they burned him, but patted my shoulder in a vaguely consoling way. "Sorry...I asked Finlay about it, and it's not possible."

"What? There's no way this hotel can be full."

"It's not. They're having to condense people...bring everybody in close, so they can save the generator. All the top floors and the other half of this one are being shut off."

"If I could trade..." I started, and then stopped. Who would want to sleep next to the murder chamber? Not even Taylor Huggins would trade rooms with me, at least not without the inducement of a nice juicy exclusive.

"I tried, Lillybet. I did try."

"You've changed, Jared."

"So have you. Natural order of things, isn't it?" he answered, his sardonic mask snapping firmly back into place. Quick as a breath that queer moment of intimacy between us was gone. "I need to go."

"Will I see you later?"

"I'll be in the bar - six PM to midnight, but I won't be able to talk to you much. Management doesn't like to see the hired help mingling socially with the guests."

It was a cruel thing to say and coldly said, but I couldn't tell which one of us he intended to hurt.

I locked and chained the door after he left. This conversation had unsettled me, almost as much as the way we had gotten along so well. I didn't want to get along well with Jared Granville. I didn't want to get on that merry-go-round again. The highs had been very good, but the lows had been too much to bear.

Remembering the revelation in the bar, I pulled out the yellowed copy of *A Man of Honor*. There was something else, too, a small metal picture frame, the kind that hold two pictures and folds shut like a book.

The left hand picture wasn't very good; it had been taken during Mardi Gras, at one of the parties. One of the less fashionable ones, I might add. Neither Kevin nor I moved in the circles that would allow us entry to one of the major balls. It had been fairly late in the evening— maybe early in the morning—and we had taken our masks off. I was wearing a ridiculously romantic ballerina's outfit, with a long net skirt that reached almost to my ankles. Kevin had been an idealized cowboy, complete with chaps and bandanna. We were both laughing and pointing at the camera.

The right hand picture was better; it was a studio portrait, the original of which sat on my dresser at home. Kevin was smiling, his eyes seeking mine even from the paper. I studied the picture dispassionately. His features were regular but undistinguished. No hawkish profile there. Sandy hair, stylishly cut, blue eyes that seemed somehow soft, a crisp white shirt, modest tie and navy blazer...all nice, all correct and all so very boring. He could be any one of a thousand men.

But was he going to be angry. He hadn't wanted me to come up here at all, at least, not without him. Kevin was one of those charming dinosaurs who thought a woman's place was in the home, and her only career her man. It might be all right if she worked as a secretary or a saleswoman or a clerk, but only as long as it didn't distract her from her main point of concentration—him.

For a while I had thought his Neanderthal attitude amusing, something that could be worked out between us...until time came to leave for here. He had a party of clients coming in for whom he wanted me to be hostess. I had committed to come here. It was the worst fight we ever had, and I suddenly realized nothing could ever be the same between us again.

Sadly, I closed the picture frame and put it in my suitcase. If nothing else, this trip had solved one of my problems. I simply could not marry Kevin. He was nice, he was kind, he was boring, and I didn't love him. Before it had gone bad, Jared and I had had something wonderful, something magic. Someday, sometime, I wanted to find that magic again and make it last. Having had the real thing once, I wasn't about to settle for second best just to keep from being alone.

Not that I would probably be alone; on top of all else, Kevin was very persistent. He would probably be at the plane when I went home again. Now that I had made up my mind definitely not to marry him, maybe we could become friends.

I should have felt free. Instead I felt very much alone

and very vulnerable.

* * *

Within half an hour I had read *A Man of Honor* over twice and knew what was wrong. I had been sublimely stupid not to see it before.

Brent Carlisle, my hero, was Jared Granville.

It was as simple as that. Having seen Jared again, the new, strangely subdued Jared, had given me back the perspective to see him as simply a man, a human with foibles and weaknesses, instead of some sort of mad super being with the power of happiness and unhappiness in his grasp.

Now I could see that Brent Carlisle was written as a sort of pseudo-Jared, which didn't suit the concept of my story at all, it was depressing; every bit of the story dealing with Brent and his reactions would have to be re-written. Blast!

I shivered. Maybe the emergency generator was doing its best, but as far as I was concerned, it was freezing. In New Orleans we had had what we considered a hard winter, but even at its worst I had never been this cold. I had never been this cold in New York. Discarding only my shoes, I had snuggled under the bedcovers like a hibernating bear while reading, and I was still cold.

Artists have long been considered crazy, and I don't guess it's been for nothing, because after all those months of dry stasis, I had to write. My fingers itched to work, even if they were beginning to turn blue. I was only glad that there was no one there to see me.

I crawled out of bed, put on my shoes and fur jacket

and the cute little woolen tam I had been unable to resist in Banff. Then, wrapping a blanket around me, I sat down at my old portable typewriter. The effect must have been similar to a literary grizzly bear.

I decided to re-key the whole manuscript. This was a new start, a fresh attempt, and I didn't want any of that old, yellowed copy's failure to taint the future. I rolled a fresh sheet of paper into the platen and said a quick prayer.

The first chapter was mainly exposition, a sort of thumbnail sketch of the Carlisle and Lamborteau families, showing how they and the Fitzwilliams—the main family in most of *A Woman of Quality*—were related. It went fairly fast, since beyond the inevitable word tinkering there was nothing to do but type it.

Even the physical act of typing felt good. It was wonderful to hit the keys and see the little type thingies jump up and down, impressing my thoughts on the page. It was a thousand times better than just sitting and dawdling, worrying and x-ing out one word after another trying to find just the right meaning.

The telephone rang half a dozen times, but I ignored it. After a while I just didn't hear it anymore.

The going got a little slower when Brent Carlisle entered the picture. I didn't want to change him too much, since a great deal of the story hinged on his charm and devil-may-care attitude, but that sharp, hurtful edge of Jared-ness, the old Jared, had to go. It was easier than anticipated, and by the time the rumbling of my stomach penetrated the fog of concentration, I had done almost three chapters.

Outside the window it was a dirty charcoal gray. At some time, I had turned on the desk lamp and it cast a weak pool of light that made the rest of the room shadowy, and scary. Of course I had locked and chained the door after Jared left, but still the effect was so spooky that I shivered and not from the pervasive cold. Locked doors and chains do not always safety make...

Locked doors.

That was what had been hovering around the outside of my consciousness.

Jane was a sensible, cautious person. She wouldn't sit in her hotel room with the door unlocked, even in a ritzy place like this. After her stalking incident—and with all the predatory aspirant writers prowling around— would she even have opened the door to a stranger? The door had been carefully locked, not broken in. I had been in the room next door, wakeful and restless. The Spa hotel's walls were sturdy, but surely I would have heard something had there been a struggle.

That would mean Jane had opened the door and invited her killer in. She had let him get close enough to drive the knife in with one sure stroke with no struggle, no outcry...

Jane not only knew her murderer, she knew him very well.

Did that mean I knew him, too?

My stomach knotted. Was it tension or simply hunger? It was six-thirty, and I made myself think it was hunger. Not the dining room, no, I might never again eat anywhere I might see a wooden handled steak knife, but perhaps I could get a sandwich or something in the coffee shop...

Did I dare go down and get something or should I order something from room service? With the emergency the staff must be almost run off its collective feet; service might take forever. On the other hand, not having to go out would be very enticing, though I would have to open the door to someone...Perhaps a tall, pale man...?

Someone I knew?

I would go down, right after I freshened up a little.

My lipstick faltered in mid-stroke as I began to think.

Of course, there was no proof that the tall, pale man Anita had seen was the murderer. It might even have been Clement, returning to his room after one of his little hunting forays. But, if that were the truth, why hadn't he said so instead of getting so upset? I could pretty well accept that it had not been he simply because he had been so upset.

Then who had Anita seen?

Of course, there were other tall, pale men, but not many of them — Gilda Wilcox's husband, for example, or some of the hotel staff. The guests, for this conference at least, were nearly all women.

Anita could have seen one of them on a perfectly innocent errand. I couldn't believe she would say such a thing just to dig at Clement. She didn't like him at all, but almost invariably and sometimes painfully she was truthful. She had seen someone, but whom?

I stared at the red lipstick and thought it looked too much like the color of blood.

Jared was tall and pale.

Golly, that was an ugly thought. We had parted

acrimoniously, and he had a strange side to his nature—as most artists do. Surely that was no reason to suspect him of murder.

I gave myself a brisk shake. This was really getting to be too much. I could accuse Jared of being a louse, a cad, a rake and a lot of other names not in common usage today, but a murderer? Ridiculous! I finished putting on my lipstick with a steady hand. There must be at least half a dozen tall, pale men in the hotel right now.

Besides, what kind of motive could Jared have for wanting to kill Jane Hall?

I was the only romance writer whom he might have the slightest desire to have done with, and even that was stretching it. Jared, a murderer? I might as well suspect Clement.

* * *

Downstairs wasn't any warmer. Between the high ceilings, marble floors and columns and the vast glass windows, it must have been quite a job to get it as warm as it was. I had discarded my blanket, but added the leather gloves I had brought for driving. Most everyone else was hardier than I. Some of them had shed their coats and a brave few—generally those with the most spectacular dresses—had even shed their sweaters.

The piano had been moved away from the windows into the middle of the room. Jared was playing a flowery version of "If I Loved You" almost losing the tune under an overload of ripples and trills. No one seemed to pay much attention, though he was receiving a fair amount of languishing and admiring looks. He had changed into a thick turtleneck sweater and an English tweed sport coat.

They looked wonderful on him.

I wondered if he remembered I was the one who had picked out that coat. We had been in Rhode Island for a concert and had had a few hours to kill before starting for home. I had seen the jacket in a store window and...

This was silly. There was no need for all these useless old memories, none at all.

Jared looked up just as I came in; his face was studiedly grim. Then he saw my costume, and unable to help himself, he began to laugh. All during that year in New York, the all-too-short and much-too-long year of our marriage, he had teased me about my intolerance for cold, calling me a thin-blooded Rebel. In retaliation I had called him a cold-hearted Yankee, but in the early days that had been funny. It was only towards the end that the words began to sting.

"Liz! Over here."

I threaded my way between the crowded tables to Bernie, glad that his was against the inner wall and away from those tall, cold windows that radiated cold the way a fire does heat. Outside, the struggling spotlights showed that the snow had slowed, but was still falling with grim determination.

Anita looked over a steaming cup of something dark and alcoholic, her glance a mixture of amazement and amusement. "Really, Elizabeth, that is the most astounding costume."

Trying for nonchalance, I stripped off my gloves as if that was what I had always planned. "I can't help it if I'm cold. You all must be part polar bear."

"Hardly. What you need is some antifreeze. You

Southerners just don't have any blood," Bernie said, signaling the waitress with an imperious gesture.

I gave the stock Southern reply. "Come down and see how you fare during one of our summers."

Within moments a steaming mug appeared in front of me. I sipped gingerly at it, knowing Bernie's penchant for eccentric concoctions.

"It's a recipe of my own," he said proudly, taking a big gulp of his. "Whipped cream on top, of course, with a coffee base and some Kahlúa and some Grand Marnier and some vodka…"

"Please," I said weakly. Luckily I had tasted it first; otherwise I wouldn't have dared. It was very warming.

"Planning to go for a walk?"

I looked up just in time to see Ralph Harcourt settling into the chair next to me.

He looked slightly less bouncy than his usual obnoxious self. I couldn't help but wonder if the weather—and perhaps, the quality of unknown writers at the conference—was getting him down. Of course, I thought ungenerously, there was always the possibility he had hoped to get some sort of deal going with Jane Hall, if he hadn't already.

And if he had, and if Bernie knew…?

"No. I'm just a little bit cold. Southerners," I added waspishly, "don't have any blood."

"Elizabeth came down too late to hear the announcement," Anita said in a smooth voice. "The manager said just a moment ago that the problem with the secondary generator was fixed and the temperature should be up to normal in a few hours."

"That's good news," I said, taking another sip. Maybe the temperature was already starting to rise, or perhaps Bernie's diabolical drink was having its effect, but I was feeling much warmer. I undid the zipper on my jacket.

"Stolen any talent yet, Harcourt?" Bernie asked. There was no trace of apprehension in his face. Either he was a very good actor or he had no faith in Harcourt's ability to get any of Wingate Romances' people away.

Ralph shrugged. "It has hardly been an auspicious time to talk business. Every time I open my mouth to talk about books, the conversation switches to murder. You'd think we were at a mystery writers' convention. Have you decided to switch over yet, my lovely?"

I didn't care for his inference that I would ever switch, nor for the cozy way he leaned over toward me. "Back off, Ralph. This isn't a time to tease."

"Is that in the best of taste, Mr. Harcourt?" asked Anita coolly, giving him a regal glance that could make hardened criminals back down.

"No, ma'am, but it's efficient. Since the conference has been canceled..."

Shocked, we all sat forward. He, the louse, sat back, having pulled our strings just as he had intended.

"What?"

"I just got it from Gilda Wilcox. They can't predict when this snow is going to stop, and combined with everything else..."

"But this is April." I cried. "It just has to be some sort of a freak storm..."

Ralph's eyes were as bright as a snake's, and just as

soulless. "I had no idea you were so anxious to speak to a bunch of tyros, Liz...Or have you found something in the mountain air that agrees with you?" He patted my hand gently.

"You are disgusting," I snapped. To my horror a fiery blush crept up towards my hairline.

"But of course. I thought we agreed on that years ago." Her fur coat draped around her shoulders, Vanessa took the last empty chair. Apparently she had heard about the heat going up, because she had chosen a peach chiffon dress that was a bit 'floaty' even for her. Next to Anita and Vanessa I felt a positive urchin.

"Hello, darling. Been allowing the plebeians to worship at the flame of your romantic genius?" Ralph asked flippantly.

Without giving Bernie a chance, Vanessa waved at the waitress. "Of course not, you horrid little man. I've been working, and don't you wish you knew on what."

"Mr. Harcourt says that the conference has been canceled," Anita said primly.

Vanessa stared first at Anita, then at Ralph. "Surely you're joking."

"Hardly. I just came from the war-room. Poor Gilda Wilcox is being harried to death by a bunch of unsold romantic housewives. She is probably the only person here who is happy that the phone lines are down, because otherwise, she'd have twice as many people yelling at her."

"I think that you are forgetting that every major author started as an unsold romantic," Bernie said with an unexpected dignity. "We can't afford to neglect upcoming talent in favor of established writers."

"I agree," Ralph said, then ignoring the fact that we were very closely surrounded by conferees, went on, "but they have to have talent, and I haven't seen any of that around here."

It was definitely getting warmer; either that, or Bernie's arcane potion was a lot stronger than he believed. I slipped out of my jacket, and pulling off my tam, tried to shake my hair back into some semblance of order.

Across the room, Jared was still smiling with amusement. When his eyes caught mine there was a moment of...of...I don't know what, but it was as tangible as a touch. It was as if he were giving me a pat on the back, a boost of encouragement. I had given him many such looks just before a particularly difficult concert; he had never before sent one to me.

His glance was so quick and unprecedented that it might have been nothing more than an illusion had he not abruptly broken off from a syrupy rendition of "Try To Remember" to begin a vigorous and rather noisy Polonaise...the Number 6 in A, I think.

Heads turned, and the babble of conversation faltered, and after a single, flawed run-through of the main theme, Jared lapsed back into some other piece of marshmallow music; I didn't know the name, but the easy listening station played it often. I didn't like it either way.

As much as I didn't want him to stop, I could appreciate why he did. Other than being completely out of place in a piano bar, the Polonaise was an extremely difficult piece, and he was massacring it. His skill was such that I don't know if anyone else besides me noticed how off his playing was, but I had heard him rehearsing it enough that every missed note was like a blow. He must not have practiced it since...since Jennifer died.

Vanessa ran her tongue over her lips in a repulsively feral gesture. "Hmmm. It seems you have indeed made a conquest, my dear. Or should I say, re-made?"

"Well, at least we know it isn't the mountains which have caught your eye," Ralph said. "At least I still have hopes of seducing you over to Peters and Worcester, if nothing else."

I glanced at Bernie and shrugged. "Sorry to disappoint all your lascivious little dreams, Ralph, but that man is not my current romance."

"Oh, come on, I've seen..." he began, but I cut him off. I was getting a little tired of telling the tale.

"He's my *ex*-husband."

The light came back into Ralph's eyes, and he leaned forward. Not that I'm such a sexpot. My mirror and the calendar disavow me of that every day, but I suppose such lacks could be overlooked if he thought he could romance himself into signing an author who had a million and a half first print run. He didn't know the agonies I was having with my second romance.

"Darling, I never knew you had been married."

"There's a great deal you don't know about me," I answered in an equally insincere tone. "And you probably wouldn't have known that if he hadn't happened to be playing here."

"You mean it was just an accident him being here?

You didn't plan this?"

Plan this? Would I ever have planned this? Who really ever wants to pick at a wound, however old? "No."

"Well, that's something. If I found that in a book I'd never believe it..."

"I think it's terribly romantic," Vanessa gushed, and I could almost predict the plot of her next book; an estranged wife and husband meet by accident and are stuck together in some romantic place—I didn't think even she could be tasteless enough to have it happen in a snowbound hotel—and rediscover their love.

At least in books things ended happily; life seldom did. I supposed I could live with it as long as no one suspected its origins.

I had to change this subject. I turned to Bernie in mute appeal. He and Anita were looking as uncomfortable as I felt.

"I liked your comment a moment ago, Bernie," I said desperately, "about how publishers had to take a chance on new writers. I'm so glad you decided to take a chance on me. Bringing out *A Woman of Quality* like you did was a big gamble...and I thank you."

Bernie smiled. "I knew you could do great things, Liz. You repaid me amply with *Sisters of Desire*. And, I expect, *Daughters of Passion* will do even better."

"And *A Man of Honor* will be the best of all." Anita spoke lightly, but in her eyes was an order.

"Anyone for another drink?" Ralph asked a little too loudly, his face disgruntled. Poor thing, he had come to sow discord and reap any discontented writers, and all he had found was a mutual admiration society. He surely wouldn't get any sort of kudos for that when he got home.

"No, thank you," Anita said in her best 'hostess' voice.

"Liz, Vanessa, you better go get your glad rags on...Time's passing."

"Changing? For what?" I asked.

"Our dinner, Liz, the Wingate dinner! We've taken a table in the Empress. It was to have been in the room at the top of the hotel, but that's been closed due to the emergency."

As soon as he spoke I remembered. One of the theoretically enticing features of the conference had been for a few of the most promising new writers to join the Wingate Romances party for dinner...sort of like a royal summons or dining at the captain's table. It wasn't Bernie's innovation, but he was acting like it was.

"I...I thought...Well, after poor Jane..."

"Jane would be the first to want us to carry on," Bernie said decisively.

"Probably she would, cold fish that she was," Ralph Harcourt said with a sour voice. "One can hardly hope that inquisitive reporter would feel the same. I can see the headlines now...'Dinner Over Death', or 'Dining With The Dead'...or something equally flattering."

"I agree, Mr. Harcourt." Anita nodded frostily. "Though I find your manner unnecessarily crude."

"Your approval flatters me, Mrs. Wingate," he replied in a tone that implied exactly the opposite.

Bernie glared. "You've canceled yours, I gather."

"Not my choice. Orders from New York."

"Peters and Worcester showing a conscience?" Bernie snorted. "Since when?"

"Some of us endeavor to improve. That's the main reason you ladies need to switch over," Harcourt said, addressing both Vanessa and me, but his attention was all on me.

"You are the complete opportunist," I murmured, but was almost drowned out by Bernie's next idea.

"If you've canceled your dinner, Harcourt, you certainly won't care if I ask your former guests to join us..."

"Bernard!"

Even Vanessa looked disturbed.

"You're kidding, aren't you?" Ralph asked. His face was ugly. "The publicity..."

"Jane was always dedicated to helping new talent, and I know she would not wish to see anyone lose their chance because of her..."

That might or might not be true; I didn't know Jane well enough to say, but Ralph Harcourt didn't have to sneer at the idea. He made an angry sort of snorting noise and got up without so much as a by your leave.

"Bernard, what are you talking about? You can't...It isn't decent."

"I can't not," Bernie snapped. "This is a God-sent opportunity. If Peters and Worcester were interested in those writers, they had to be good. If Wingate Romances is to survive, we must have a broad base of good writers to fill the vacancy Jane left. Now, I've got to go talk to Gilda Wilcox, find out who they were and invite them to join us before Harcourt can turn things around."

It was as if he had slapped Anita. Normally, Bernie worshipped his wife, and none of us had ever heard him speak so harshly to her before. Anita went alarmingly pale, with only a single bright spot of color on each cheek. She gripped her mug until her knuckles went white, but when she spoke her voice was cool and calm.

"If that is the way you wish it, Bernard."

"Aren't you going to change, honey? Put on that new dress you bought?"

Anita shook her head. "I don't think so. If we must go on with it, we don't want it to be too formal...because of poor Jane."

Anita was being modest; as usual, she looked glorious in a deceptively simple floor length shirtwaist of claret-colored silk and a ransom of grayish pearls. About the only thing for which she would not be formal enough was a coronation.

"We will do it just as we planned," Bernard said

"He is right, you know," Vanessa said, draining her mug and looking around hopefully. "We must go on. A strong Wingate Romances would be the best memorial for poor Jane."

"I wonder if the Mounties have made any progress," I murmured. Everyone was being so civilized and so proper, and talking as if Jane had simply passed away. She had been murdered; someone had deliberately taken her life and was still on the loose.

"We're all distressed," Anita replied in a surprisingly gentle voice. "And I for one am more than a little frightened, but there is nothing to be gained by panicking."

"There's a murderer among us," I said.

"You're being ghoulish," Vanessa replied, waving her empty mug at the waitress.

"You didn't see her lying there all covered with blood..." All of a sudden I did again, her dress wet, her eyes open and staring....

"I'm so sorry you were the one who had to discover her," Anita said soothingly, covering my shaking hand with her own. "But the Mounties are here. Surely we're safe with them. Besides," she added with a tight little grin, "if Bernard wants things to go as he planned, things will go as he planned, no matter what."

"I know it seems heartless, Liz, but this is an emergency. If we want Wingate Romances to survive, we've got to strike while we can."

"I understand that...I just can't forget that there is a murderer loose."

"And the Mounties will find him," Bernard said, patting my shoulder. "Jane was a very private woman, you know. There may have been a reason for that."

Vanessa looked up from her fresh mug. There was a slight rime of whipped cream on her upper lip. "You know, there really was a lot we didn't know about her. She could have all kinds of enemies. The motive had to be something from her private life...she had too many fans and was too well respected professionally."

It was a tribute to both women that Vanessa's tribute sounded neither snide nor jealous.

"That's what I mean," Bernie said, his face grim. "None of us know anything about her private life. Remember that nut who stalked her? Does anyone know anything about any private problem? For that matter, do any of you have any secrets?"

For an uncomfortable moment everyone's eyes shifted to me, probably just because I hadn't told anyone I had once been married. Then Vanessa unknowingly rescued me. The idea that she might be in danger obviously hadn't occurred to her, and she gulped. "No...Nothing, Thank God."

"Liz?"

"Nothing."

"Do either of you know if Clement...Where is Clement?"

Perhaps that was what had been making me uneasy ever since I had come down. It was rare not to find Clement in some bar at this hour, and this was the only bar open. There were ten thousand things he could be doing, but apparently everyone's mind leapt to the same horrible possibility as mine.

"I don't know," Vanessa said. Her mug was shaking slightly. Her face had gone pasty white and on her cheeks two splotches of rouge stood out like smears of blood. "Do you suppose...?"

"Oh, certainly not." Anita was brisk. We mustn't let our nerves run away from us. Clement Wallingford is not a child."

"Neither was Jane," Vanessa said morbidly.

"Don't be ridiculous." I spoke with an assurance I didn't really feel. "We mustn't be like children scaring ourselves in the dark. Clement probably found some...someone to talk to," I ended lamely.

"Thank you, Elizabeth. I appreciate your delicacy,

but we can all surmise what sort of disgusting activity that man is up to." Anita's agitation showed in her disregard for grammar. Normally she was much more precise than any of the writers her husband published.

"Who saw him last?" Bernie asked sensibly. "Did he say anything after we left the tea table this afternoon?"

I shook my head. "He was still with Vanessa when I left. There were a bunch of conferees coming for Vanessa's autograph, so I went upstairs to work."

Something very ugly entered Vanessa's heavily made-up eyes. Funny, I had never noticed how small and hard they were before. "You aren't going to involve me in this."

"No one is trying to involve you in anything, Vanessa." Now Bernie was pacific. "I just want to know the last time you saw him, and if he said anything."

"The last time I saw him was at tea. Liz had just gone upstairs, and I was talking to a few of my fans. Clement was being his usual vulgar self; I saw it was upsetting the ladies, so I asked him to leave. He was very rude."

"Did he leave?" I asked.

"Only after saying some absolutely unforgivable things."

"Did you see which way he went?" Now Bernie was grabbing at straws.

"Toward the elevators. I don't know if he went upstairs or not, though. My attention was on my fans," Vanessa added sententiously.

"So no one has seen him since tea." Bernie rubbed his chin thoughtfully.

"I was in my room all afternoon," I said slowly, though no one had asked, trying to remember anything out of the circle of my immediate memories and coming up with nothing. "I worked most of the time, so he could have come and gone half-a-dozen times, and I wouldn't have noticed."

"If he went to his own room," Vanessa added spitefully.

"Sitting around and speculating like this is ridiculous," Bernie said. "I'm going to go call him."

"Bernard!" Outraged, Anita sat forward, her fists clenched. "That is obscene. It is bad enough that man is the way he is without you going poking and prodding into something that should be private."

"One of our friends has been murdered, Anita. I can't think there is any connection, but it is a chance I don't care to take. If Clement has found a...a friend, all is well and good."

"Disgusting, you mean."

"That isn't for us to say. You don't have to be so judgmental all the time." Bernie stopped abruptly, aware that concentric ripples of interest were turning heads toward them. He lowered his voice to a whisper. "You wait here; I will go call his room. You don't have to be a part of anything."

"Bernard...." The single word was like a sliver of ice.

I should have gone upstairs; I needed to dress if we were going to go through with this horrible charade of a dinner, but I simply could not make myself get up. To leave the light and companionship of the bar, even if Anita were in as bad a snit as I had ever seen, and go up that small elevator and through that shadowy hall to an empty room next to where Jane...I just couldn't.

I tried to catch Jared's eye, hoping for another look of confidence, but the piano was surrounded by a giggling group of conferees. Not a one of them was under forty or size fourteen, yet all of them were acting like high school girls on a senior trip. Poor Jared would be overwhelmed.

With a grim casualness the three of us chatted determinedly on several subjects; Anita spoke with determined sophistication of an art show she had seen. Vanessa contributed what at some other time might have been an amusing anecdote about one of her speaking engagements. My poor contribution was a description of the last Mardi Gras. Another full mug in her hand, Vanessa listened with more interest than Anita, and then fuzzily invited herself down for next year, saying it would make a charming background for a story she had in mind. I didn't have the heart to tell her that Mardi Gras was hopelessly overdone; most of what Vanessa did was too.

Jared played on, this time a medley of Rodgers and Hammerstein tunes. He had always hated Rodgers and Hammerstein, calling them the fast food of the music business and berating me because I thought "Some Enchanted Evening" was one of the most beautiful songs ever written. It seemed that during that unbearably long time he played every tune R&H had ever written except "Some Enchanted Evening".

Then he quit playing and walked over to the table, leaving his fan club behind. I didn't know if I were glad to see him or not. Heaven knows we three women had run out of light chatter, but I didn't really like the idea of mixing my past life and my present one.

"I'm glad to see you finally decided to stop being a polar bear," he said lightly enough, but there was concern in his eyes.

"One of Bernie's concoctions would heat up Chicago," I returned flippantly.

"Are you supposed to leave the piano?" Vanessa asked ingenuously, her voice only slightly slurred. "You play so prettily."

Prettily. A funny kind of description for a pianist who had won almost every competition going, then garnered an equal number of kudos from critics all over the world. I waited for Jared to blow up.

He didn't. He merely shrugged and laughed. "Even piano players get to take breaks now and then..."

"Mrs. Wingate?" A bellboy managed to address all three of us women impartially. He was a good-looking kid who seemed to belong more out on the ski slopes than in the nauseating fake *lederhosen* uniform of knee britches and embroidered braces that was *de rigueur* for all male employees. Vanessa was almost salivating.

"I am she," Anita said in a strained voice.

"Your husband is upstairs, ma'am. He sent me to ask you and Miss Allison and Miss Mangold if you would please come with me."

He was sweating.

It was still barely above freezing in here, and he was sweating.

My hands began to shake; I didn't realize how obviously until Jared reached down to clasp them in his own. I wished he hadn't; it drew attention, and that wasn't desirable for either of us. Neither did I want to think about what it might mean, no matter how comforting it was at the moment. I didn't want to depend on Jared Granville for anything, even comforting. I had before, and he had let me down many times. Still, I didn't move, and told myself it was only because there was no way to pull away without attracting undue notice.

"Bernard wants me...upstairs?"

"And me?" Vanessa asked. They both looked frightened.

I couldn't speak.

"Now, if you please, ma'am."

We all four stood as if a drunken puppeteer pulled crazily on our strings. Jared still held my hands, but now I was clinging to him so tightly he couldn't have pulled away.

"I'll go with you," he said and his fingers pressed heavily against mine in secret confirmation.

As if I could have defied him. Without his support I might have fallen down. I was staggering under the weight of unwanted understanding. There could be only one reason why Bernie would send for us so peremptorily, why a healthy young man should be white-faced and sweating in a frigid room.

It had happened again.

Chapter Seven

They were waiting for us in Clement's room. It almost seemed as if poor Jane's death were being re-enacted in a macabre way, save that this time it was Clement's body sprawled ungracefully on the floor. Mercifully, someone had had the charity to throw the bedspread over his lanky, ungraceful form, but even from under that covering a lip of blood had escaped. Still vivid red, it looked incongruously bright and gay in that grim room.

The harsh overhead light gave an eerie feeling of unreality. In the corner the two grim-faced Mounties talked in low tones. A young maid hunched in the armchair, her face buried in her apron, sobbing lustily. Bernie, his face a ghastly white, sat on the edge of the bed and stared blankly at nothing. Somehow, he had never looked so small or so old before.

Cooing little sounds of distress, Anita ignored the stiffening thing that had been Clement and flew to her husband, wrapping her arms around him. They clung together like frightened children.

For once in her life Vanessa was struck dumb, and she staggered slightly as Officer Hunter, seeing her distress, gently seated her on the desk chair. The greenish tinge of her skin clashed with her peach dress.

If Jared hadn't been holding me tightly I would have slid to the floor in a boneless lump. Heaven knew I hadn't particularly liked Clement Wallingford, but that was no reason to want to see him twisted and dead.

He had been tall, so tall that the spread didn't quite cover him. The sole of one brown shoe peeked out through the tangled fringe.

Without warning I began to shake. Jared pulled me against him, turning my head with his cold hand until it was familiarly buried in his shoulder. I was glad; I couldn't pull my eyes from the horrid stillness that had once been Clement. He had been obnoxious and vulgar, but he had been so full of life and energy that I couldn't believe he was so motionless.

"Hush, Lillybet, hush," Jared crooned, and I realized I must have been babbling. His hand made slow circles in the middle of my back.

"I'm ruined," Bernie said suddenly in lugubrious tones. "First Jane, now Clement...two of my top writers...without them we're ruined..."

"Darling..." Anita's face creased with worry as she tried to comfort her husband. For the first time she really looked old, and oddly, more human. "Don't say that. It's terrible, but we aren't ruined. We still have the publishing house..."

Eyes wide with drunken terror, Vanessa started to hiccough with fear. She was clinging to Officer Walter's hand as if she were drowning. Her aura of glamour had fallen away, leaving only an aging, over painted woman.

"I think..." Vanessa said fuzzily, "...that I am going to be sick." Then she lost all of Bernie's concoction on the floral patterned carpet.

"Pete," Jared asked in a calm voice, "why don't you tell us what you know."

The harassed Mountie looked grateful that there was at least one sensible person in the room. Poor man, he appeared to be completely out of his depth. "Murder. Without question. Again. Mr. Wingate called us after he couldn't get Mr. Wallingford to answer the phone or a knock. We got the maid to open the door. We found him dead on the floor."

How simple it sounded when boiled down to a few words. It was almost exactly the same story I had told, but those spare words could never convey the multitude of feelings behind it, for me or for Bernie. I felt badly enough, but Bernie looked ghastly.

"Mr. Wallingford was stabbed. Sharp instrument."

"Which was...?" I didn't recognize my own voice. I couldn't tell you why I asked; in my heart of hearts I already knew the answer.

"A steak knife." The officer motioned to a plastic bag on the dresser. "Looks just like the other one."

"So whoever did this killed Jane, too?" Bernie asked in a breathy squeak. His face was so drawn and gray I couldn't help wondering about his heart. He wasn't all that young any more.

Also, he was innocent of both murders. Bernie was not that good an actor.

"Possibly. Probably, but we can't say for sure until we prove it."

"Any other clues?" Jared asked.

"None. Just the knife and I'll bet my next paycheck it's been wiped clean." Sergeant Hunter shook his head angrily. "Okay, do any of you know anyone who might have wanted to kill Wallingford?"

"He was a disgusting man," Anita said with disdain. "His behavior was totally uncalled for under any circumstances. He wore his disgrace like a badge."

"His disgrace?" the Mountie asked quickly. He wasn't used to Anita or her particular thought processes.

"He was a homosexual." She pronounced the word as if it alone could defile.

"Oh," said Hunter.

"Still," Anita added, visibly struggling to be fair, "I cannot see where that, however immoral, could be grounds for murder. I cannot think of anyone who liked him, but neither can I think of anyone who disliked him enough to kill him."

"There was one," I murmured.

"Perhaps he found a...person of similar tastes. Everyone knows that kind of pervert attracts evil."

"And how would that explain Miss Hall's death, Mrs. Wingate?"

That silenced Anita, but not Jared. "That's not a bad idea, Pete. A copycat killing?"

"Good thinking, Jerry, except that we haven't released what kind of knife Miss Hall was stabbed with...no one knows except a few people."

"Us?" I asked.

"Yes." Sergeant Hunter dug out his notebook and pen. "All right, folks, let's get this over with..."

"Must we remain in here?" Anita snapped. "My husband..."

"I'm all right, honey," Bernie muttered, but it wasn't true. He looked dreadful.

"I agree...This place is awful...I must lie down...I'm

ill..." Vanessa still looked green, though there could be no alcohol nor anything else left in her stomach. Thankfully someone had tossed a towel over her mess.

"No, you are not. You've had a dreadful shock." Ignoring Vanessa, Anita spoke directly to her husband, and then turned her imperious gaze to Hunter. "Why can't you postpone this?"

"Because we can't, ma'am."

"Then at least let us move to another room."

In less than an instant Hunter's gaze flicked over each of us, and I revised my opinion about him being out of his depth. There was something in that quick look that bespoke a ruthless, clever professional.

"We are trying to avoid a panic, Mrs. Wingate. The less upheaval about this, the better. Now when was the last time you saw Mr. Wallingford?"

It was a travesty of our conversation in the bar. One by one we recounted our afternoons while Sergeant Hunter made quick notes.

"Can anyone verify that you were working in your room all afternoon, Miss MacAllister?"

I shook my head slowly. "No...I didn't speak to anyone."

"I can," Jared said simply, and I stared at him in surprise. "Well, at least part of it. I got worried, so I came up here to see if she were all right."

"Jared..."

"So you were on this floor this afternoon. When?"

"I don't remember the time exactly, about five, five-thirty maybe. I heard her working."

"You could hear her working?"

"My typewriter is old; it's not one of the silent kind. Besides, I read my scenes aloud as I finish them," I said almost hesitantly, as one does when revealing something intensely personal. "It's an old habit."

"And you were sure she was alone?" Hunter asked. "She was talking to herself, not someone else?"

"Positive," Jared replied. "She was taking both parts."

Inwardly I gulped. Just what had he heard? I had written some pretty emotional stuff that afternoon. Living alone, I had become unaccustomed to modulating my voice, but still, I must have been really involved to make my voice heard beyond the Spa hotel's thick doors.

"Do you know what time he came up, Miss MacAllister?"

"She didn't know I was there," Jared said quickly. "I didn't knock."

"Why?" Hunter's question was like a whip crack.

"Because I could hear her working inside. I didn't want to disturb her."

The answer seemed to satisfy the police, but not me. Jared had never been reticent about disturbing my work whenever it suited his purpose. It had been a painful point of contention between us.

Jared was a tall, pale man.

Had he been using me for an alibi? Why? If he hadn't mentioned it, probably no one would have thought he had been on the floor. Unless someone had seen him...

On the other hand, had he been trying to give me an alibi? Did he honestly believe anyone could think me capable of murder?

I stared up at his strong face without understanding. Although the planes and lines of his face were heart-wrenchingly familiar, it was like looking at a stranger. We had been married for a little over a year, and he had occupied a great deal of my thoughts for the two and a half years we had been apart, and I still knew nothing about him. I pulled away from him and stood a little straighter.

Something else. Now we knew that the tall, pale man Anita had seen had not been Clement.

Vanessa was telling her story now. Although she was still pale with lipstick clownishly smeared around her mouth, she looked less ghastly. She wasn't up to her usual flowery speeches, which probably made it easier for Sergeant Hunter. Neither had she released her stranglehold on Officer Walters' hand, much to that young man's embarrassment.

At last the ordeal was over. Sergeant Hunter folded up his notebook and stuffed it into his pocket. All thoughts of food and the dinner and the conference forgotten, I started to dream of locking myself in my room, taking a long hot soaking bath and not seeing anyone until morning, at least. Maybe by then the snow would have magically disappeared, and murder investigation or no, I would head directly back to New Orleans. If the police wanted to talk to me, they could jolly well do so on my own nice, warm, safe patio.

"All right," Hunter said, and his eyes were cold, "let's go on. What did you have planned for tonight?"

I would have bet he already knew the answer.

"A dinner." Bernie's voice was weak but still bitter. "A dinner to try to recruit writers for Wingate Romances. Wingate Romances! I'm ruined..."

"Of course, now that is out of the question..."

"I'm sorry, Mrs. Wingate, but it isn't. I must ask you to go on with your plans as you had intended."

Sergeant Hunter's pronouncement brought a wail of protest from all of us.

"You must be joking."

"No, I truly want you go on with your dinner as planned. I understand it will be rough on all of you, but you don't really have a choice. There are over a hundred and fifty people here, and the news of one murder has made them jumpy. The news of a second might panic them completely, and we must avoid that at all costs. Is that clear?"

"No," Jared said abruptly. "Shouldn't they be told so they can protect themselves?"

"And how are they going to do that? No, you all are going to do exactly as I say." There was no room for debate in that cold, precise voice.

"A dinner for Wingate Romances," Bernie said. His color was coming back, and he looked almost normal again. You could almost hear the wheels of business creaking in his head. "Now, I really have to get hold of those Peters and Worcester people...before they hear about this."

"No one is to hear of this, Mr. Wingate."

"You cannot ask it of us," Anita said at her most regal. "It is inhuman. My husband is not at all well."

"I am sorry, Mrs. Wingate, but I must insist. You

must all act as normally as possible."

"You are going to use us as lures?" Vanessa asked shrilly, pulling the luckless officer even closer. He looked like he was having trouble breathing. "Targets?'

"No, Miss Mangold, that's not what I mean at all. I want you to act as normally as possible while Officer Walters and I watch everyone else's reaction. If the killer doesn't think that we know about Mr. Wallingford's death, he—or she—might make some slip."

Anita's eyes widened with horror. "You think this fiend might be a woman?"

"It's possible, Mrs. Wingate. It doesn't really take much strength to stab a person. And the killer knows just where to put the knife for maximum effect. One thrust..."

"Please," I said weakly, revolted. Jared pulled me back into his arms and resumed the slow rubbing of my back. I didn't resist; his support was comforting...just as long as I didn't allow myself to expect it.

"So you think our behaving normally might unmask the killer," Bernie said slowly.

"He—or she—has to make a mistake soon, sir."

"And just you two men are going to watch everyone?" Anita asked with patent disbelief.

"We will do our best, ma'am."

"Finlay will put hotel security under your command..." Jared began, but when the sergeant glared fiercely at him, it was obvious that he had already done so. It wasn't like Jared to state the obvious. Was he trying to warn someone?

"All right, we'll do it." Bernie squared his jaw in a credible imitation of John Wayne urging on the troops in face of unspeakable odds. "Come on, everyone. If we're going to have a successful dinner we've got a lot to do and not much time to do it in."

"Bernard, are you mad? This man is *killing* people."

"Bernie!" Vanessa and I wailed in unaccustomed unison.

"Do you think that is wise, Mr. Wingate?" Jared asked.

"Nobody will be safe until this monster is caught," Bernie said with his old assurance. "Besides, it's the only way I can see to save Wingate Romances."

"Bernie, I can't." Vanessa wailed. Mascara and eyeliner were streaking down her face leaving lines like gouges. She had moved her grip up to Officer Walters' elbow; it looked like she was trying to pull him into her lap.

"Bernard, I will not have you exposing any of us to danger."

"We'll be watching, Miss Mangold, Mrs. Wingate. You couldn't be safer."

"As I recall, Sergeant Hunter, you said something very similar to that just after we found poor Jane."

The sergeant looked uncomfortable; most people did when Anita's displeasure was focused on them. At least his arguments made sense. If we all kept our heads and stayed together we could protect each other.

"There is safety in numbers," I said slowly.

Sergeant Hunter sent me an appraising glance. "You're right, Miss MacAllister. Now, we'll escort all of you to your rooms so you can get ready. When did you have the dinner planned?"

"Nine o'clock, sharp," Anita replied. "Officer..."

"Sergeant, Mrs. Wingate. Sergeant Hunter."

"Sergeant, what if while you're watching us, someone else gets killed?"

"That is a possibility, Ma'am, but so far both murders have been Wingate writers. However, you can be sure we'll be keeping an eye on everyone."

"Someone is obviously trying to destroy me." Bernie muttered intensely.

"Surely you don't think that Harcourt man..." Anita gasped. "He's a boor, obviously, but a murderer?"

"That doesn't make sense, Anita," I said, my voice only slightly muffled by Jared's shoulder. "I agree Ralph Harcourt is a drip, but if he were behind the murders, he would have killed Bernie. Why would he kill the very writers he is trying to steal?"

"Bernard..." Her eyes panicky, Anita wrapped her arms protectively around her husband as if to ward off any attacks.

"See? I said someone was trying to destroy me."

"Sound thinking, Miss MacAllister," Officer Walters said. He was trying less and less gently to extricate himself from Vanessa's clutches and in the process resembled Laocoön in the snake's unrelenting grip.

"They're going to kill me!" Vanessa wailed, gripping the Mountie until he yelped.

"Please, Miss Mangold," the sergeant said in the same professional tone. "My main theory is that some sort of psychopath is behind this, some frustrated writer who feels that Miss Hall and Mr. Wallingford were receiving attentions he — or she — should get. Have you rejected many writers, Mr. Wingate?"

Bernie laughed. It was shocking in that hushed room of death, and I found myself waiting for Clement's acid comment, but Clement was cold and stiff and dead and would never make nastily amusing remarks about anything ever again.

"Rejected many writers? Sergeant, you don't know what you're saying. Everybody who has ever read a book thinks they can write one and most of them have tried. I've rejected as many fifty writers in a week. Rejected writers...My God!"

"And this is a conference for novice writers," the sergeant muttered despondently. "That makes practically everyone in the hotel a suspect."

"Pete," Jared said slowly, speaking for the first time in a long while. His hand had stopped rubbing my back and was firmly clamped around my waist. "I hate to be the one to bring it up, but there's one other possibility."

"Which is?"

"We may be missing the motive for his murder. What if someone killed Jane Hall for their own reasons, then when Elizabeth and Wallingford found her body, realized that there was something incriminating left behind?" Jared stopped, waiting for agreement.

"Go on."

"That means they may have seen something that, although they don't realize it, would incriminate the murderer."

Now it was obvious where he was going. I drew a shaky breath.

"If that's true," Jared went on, "that means Elizabeth

is to be the next victim."

I wished he hadn't said that. Oh, did I ever wish he hadn't said that.

"But I've told you all everything," I wailed. "I don't know anything."

"Maybe the killer thinks you do," Jared murmured.

"Please," I said in a very little voice, "rub my back." Then, after a moment, "What about the maid who opened the door? If that's true, she's in danger, too."

"She's under protection," Sergeant Hunter said shortly, confirming my impression that he had thought of this horrid possibility long before Jared had.

"Then why isn't Elizabeth under the same protection?" Jared growled.

"Look, Jerry, if we're going to catch this killer..."

"I will not have Elizabeth used as bait!" Jared roared, and the whole room stared at him. For the first time since we had been here he sounded like the old temperamental Jared. While it was good to have him champion me, it was also sort of sad; leopards don't really change their spots.

"Look, Jerry, I know you're worried about her, but she will be safer here with us looking out for her. Like she said herself, there's safety in numbers."

Me and my big mouth.

"Now, I want all of you to stay in your rooms until one of us comes to get you."

"Is such a course not a little obvious, Sergeant? I mean, if this is supposed to be kept secret..."

Pete Hunter nodded thoughtfully. "You're right, Mrs. Wingate, but to minimize the risk factor..."

"I'll do escort duty if you like, Pete."

"Okay, Jerry," the officer said slowly. "No one would notice anything unusual if you were with the party."

Anita had seen a tall, pale man...

"How do we know," Vanessa asked in a tight voice, eerily picking up on my thoughts, "that he isn't the murderer?"

"Vanessa, the only writer he would want to murder would be me," I said too quickly. "And I trust him."

"You do?" Jared asked softly.

"Not to murder me, I do."

Had it been anyone but Jared I would have sworn he looked crestfallen.

"Then that's settled. We'll check your rooms then Jerry can come for all of you..."

"I need to be downstairs," Bernie said.

"Bernard!"

"Anita, if I don't make contact with some more good writers soon, Wingate Romances will be dead before our first printing release. Go on with the police and this Mr...."

"Granville. Jared Granville."

"Mr. Granville can bring you down with Liz and Vanessa." Bernie gripped her hand tightly. "Anita, I'm fighting for Wingate Romances."

Her face tight, Anita nodded slowly. "If you must, dear."

"I'll hurry...Have my things laid out for me, would you, dear? I won't have much time to change."

Officer Walters had finally managed to detach

himself from Vanessa; he looked inexpressibly relieved. He opened the door, and the atmosphere in the room changed subtly; it ceased to be academic. Now the risk was real.

As Jared put his hand on my waist and propelled me toward the door I realized that one thing had changed, and no one had mentioned it. The somewhat comforting idea that Jane's murder had been a personal thing; something that was specific to her and remote from the rest of us, had been shattered.

Now, all of us were not only suspects, we were potential victims.

* * *

"Jared...stay with me." There was a pleading note in my voice I didn't like.

He paused at my door. Officer Walters had done a quick search while we all had waited in the hall, then the party had gone on down to Vanessa's room. There had been nothing unusual, as expected, but I didn't want to be alone, even in an empty room.

"You'll be all right, Lillybet... Elizabeth." He almost covered his mistake. His old pet name for me carried a lot of baggage for both of us. "I've got to go down and talk to Finlay."

"Can't the Mounties explain to him?"

"Yes, but I've got to tell him about why I left the lounge in the first place. And see if I still have a job. Now, chain the door behind me, and don't open it until you hear me knock. I'll be back to take you and the others down in twenty minutes."

I did chain the door, muttering angrily as I did. What

a time for him to get all noble and honorable. How could he even think of what the manager would think when I was so scared and lonely and needed him with me?

Why should I ever have thought he would do anything different but whatever pleased him at any given moment?

After all this time, why was I thinking I needed Jared?

What a weak, stupid, feminine thing to do. It hadn't done me any good two years before, and it wouldn't do me any good now.

The cold must be warping my brain. He might have been behaving strangely, but he was still Jared Granville, even if he were calling himself Jerry Grant.

Anger gave me strength. I skinned out of my jeans and sweater and pulled on the special dress I had bought for this dinner. Never in my life had I owned such a glamorous gown, not even for the glitziest of Jared's concerts. Then he had always been the center of attention and didn't want anyone to forget it even for a minute. I had usually worn something black or some other neutral, unobtrusive color. My dresses had always been costly, well cut and elegant, but never flashy.

This was flashy.

I smoothed the clingy material over my hips. This certainly made up for all those expensively drab ones. I had thought to stand out as one of the Wingate Fabulous Four; now its glitter would give me courage. It had cost much too much, but the off-the-shoulder column of opalescent silver sequins made me feel more glamorous than I ever had before. I had even bought a shell-shaped silver bag with a moonstone-studded clasp to go with it. It was an outfit to transform one.

With my hair carelessly swept up and held with heavy silver combs, a good dose of make-up and the chandelier crystal earrings, I felt equal to anything.

Except cold. I draped my unfortunately sporty jacket around my shoulders and vaguely wished for at least a silver chinchilla cape. One last spray of perfume, and I was ready.

The clock showed that the twenty minutes were almost up. Now my fears seemed to have shrunk to manageable size. Just because someone had murdered Jane and Clement, it didn't necessary follow that the same someone had killed them both. Someone could have killed Jane for their own reasons, then someone else could have had taken advantage of the situation to get rid of Clement for totally different reasons. The fact that they used the same weapon could be merely a coincidence. The steak knives were appallingly available, easy to conceal and efficient. Clement's tongue had been wicked enough to earn him enemies.

Now that I was dressed and ready the waiting began to chafe. This room was suddenly unbearably small. Even the weather was closing in, grayish white and opaque. Outside the window, the snow still drifted down, fingering at the glass.

What a coward I was to sit and wait like a bump on a log when all I had to do was walk a little way down the hall, punch the elevator button and ride down to join the crowds. It was simple. I had done it many times before.

I couldn't do it now.

The phone in the bar rang four times before a harried-sounded waitress answered. They must be doing quite a bit of business tonight.

"Bar."

"May I speak to Jared...Jerry Grant, please?"

"He's not here."

He must be on his way. He had always been infuriatingly prompt. I hung up, as there was a sharp, staccato knock on Vanessa's door. Finally! Now I could leave this room that had become a prison. I breathed deeply as I picked up my purse, and the incipient panic receded. Jared had often teased me, sometimes kindly, sometimes not, about my claustrophobia, but it was something very real to me.

That his first knock had been on Vanessa's door didn't surprise me. After my babyish plea for him to stay he wouldn't want to risk another emotional scene. Besides, Vanessa's room was nearer the elevators.

I didn't wait for him to knock on my door. I stepped out into the dim hallway; turning to be sure I locked the door behind me.

"I'm ready, Jared. I thought you'd never..."

The dim hallway exploded into blackness, and I was falling, falling....

Janis Susan May

Chapter Eight

Amazing how when you get hit on the head it makes your stomach feel all queasy. I had thought that when you got knocked out there was a sunburst of pain at the base of your skull; I'd even written that into one of my books, but it wasn't true. Oh, my head hurt, right enough, but it was only after I awoke. I guess you really don't feel the blow that gets you.

"Lillybet! Lillybet!" It sounded like Jared was calling me from the bottom of a well. Where on earth was he?

For that matter, where was I?

"Lillybet..." One of Jared's arms was around me while his other hand ran up and down my body. "I can't find any stab wounds..."

"Thank Heavens!" That was Anita. She sounded upset.

"What's happening?" I croaked, and now it sounded as if I were the one in a well. The effort of speaking was like banging my head against a wall.

"It's all right now, Lillybet. Just lie still."

Jared was calling me Lillybet again. He really was. I hadn't been hit hard enough to imagine that.

"Thank God you're still alive, Elizabeth." Anita shrilled, sending little daggers of pain through my head. "Are you hurt?"

I let my mind run down my body. The rest of me appeared to be in great shape compared to my throbbing head and rolling stomach. Reluctantly, and against my

158

better judgment, I opened my eyes and in doing so came to full consciousness. I was tenderly cradled in Jared's arms. Above me his worried face swam like an undernourished parody of a full moon. One of the hallway lights gave him a halo. I thought about laughing at the incongruity, but it would take too much energy. Besides, Jared looked much too worried.

"Are you all right, Lillybet?"

"No. My head hurts, and I feel like I'm going to throw up, and what in the world am I doing lying on the hall floor?"

His face lightened. "You're all right."

Anita made a sound of disgust. "She needs a doctor. Will someone...?"

Trust Anita to make this into a circus. I might ache, but I knew I was all right. Besides, I hated doctors. "No, don't... I'm fine, I really am..."

"At least let me look at your head..." That was Anita. She was already reaching toward me.

I pushed her hands away.

Jared gripped me more firmly. "Maybe you should let her..."

Anita as a nurse was not something I wanted to think about. "No. I'm all right, I tell you. Stop grabbing at me."

Maybe it was nothing more than self-hypnosis, but I really was starting to feel better. My head still ached, but my stomach was once again serene and very conscious of being empty.

Sergeant Hunter's face swam into view. Good Heavens, who else was here?

"Let's take her into her room, Jerry. Where's the key?"

"It is in the lock." Anita sounded exasperated. "Officer..."

"Sergeant, Ma'am."

"Well, then, Sergeant, why aren't you doing something about finding the person who committed this atrocity? No thanks to you Elizabeth wasn't killed."

"What we need is to find out what she was doing in the hall, Mrs. Wingate. Then maybe we can start finding out who did it." He sounded very harassed.

The import of their words sank in. I was alive, and although somewhat dented around the edges, unharmed, all with no effort on my part. It was frightening.

A vague idea began to flicker in my brain.

"What's the matter, Lillybet?"

Jared's perceptiveness was surprising; I wasn't aware of having moved. I didn't dare trust this new, strange incarnation of the man who had been my husband, especially with an idea so strange and amorphous. Besides, the idea of talking wasn't too pleasant. My mouth felt as if it had been rinsed with Novocain.

"They're so loud..."

"It's all right, Honey. We're going to let you lie down." Jared's voice was deep and calming. "We're going to let you rest."

Then the weirdest thing of all happened; Jared picked me up, easily, effortlessly, as if I were a child. Jared had never — Never! — picked me up before, not even over the threshold on our wedding night. For that matter, he never picked up anything heavier than a musical score. His hands were his music, he said time and time again, and he would not endanger them. I never objected to carrying the groceries, but his attitude had always smacked of paranoia to me.

And now he was carrying me. That alone was enough to blow away the last clinging webs of darkness. Gently, he laid me down on the bed, then propped himself at the head, so that I leaned back as much against him as the pillows. Beneath my cheek I could feel his heart beating, strong and stately as a pavane.

The room seemed to be full of people. Jared and Anita and the two Mounties and Vanessa...It was quite a party. I wished I had put away the notebook so blatantly labeled *A Man of Honor*. Bernie would have a fit that I was working on it instead of *Daughters of Passion*.

"I have the feeling of coming in on the middle of the movie. Would somebody please tell me what happened?"

"Why don't you tell us what you remember first, Miss MacAllister?" The sergeant had his pad ready.

"All right," I said, and in as simple a way possible told them what happened. The only thing that raised an eyebrow was when I got to the part where I didn't want to stay in the room one more minute. Sergeant Hunter looked questioningly towards Jared.

"That's right, Pete. Elizabeth never could stand to be cooped up. It's a form of claustrophobia."

The Mountie's expression was eloquent about what he thought of slightly neurotic women in the middle of a murder investigation, but he let me go on until I reached the part about bending over to lock the door.

"And that's all?"

"That's all. I started to lock the door, and the next think I knew I was laying on the floor and everyone was shouting."

Vanessa, pale and shaky to begin with, was now all but gobbling with horror. "You mean that wasn't you knocking at my door? You weren't trying to get help?"

If I were seeking help from a physical attack, the last person I would run to would be Vanessa, but I couldn't say that. "No, I didn't have time. I bent over to lock the door and..." I tried to shrug, but it hurt.

Suddenly Vanessa was trying to scream, but no sound came out, and that made it the more horrible. She could only manage a few choked gurgles, sounding more like a teakettle coming to a boil than a woman on the verge of hysterics.

"Vanessa!" Anita snapped and laid a businesslike hand hard across her cheek. "Stop that."

Even though she was wearing a beautiful gown of drifty pink chiffon and a spectacular scattering of jewels, there was nothing pretty about Vanessa now. The horrible burbling had stopped, but her face looked ravaged as if by a long illness.

"But don't you see? I'm the next victim! Me! He wants to kill me. The killer was knocking at *my* door. If I had opened it..."

"Why didn't you answer your door, Miss Mangold?" Sergeant Hunter asked quietly.

"I...I..."

"Did you know who was out there? Did you have

162

any reason not to open the door?"

"I was still putting on my make-up. I...I..." The burbling began again, and in the next breath, screaming. This time it was genuine hysteria, perhaps the first true emotion she had felt in years; she didn't even have enough control to grab for Officer Walters, though he stood ready to catch her if she fell.

Not even Anita's second slap did any good. She gave a quiet order and with the younger Mountie's help got Vanessa started toward the door.

"What's happened?" Gray-faced, Bernie peeked through the door. "Anita..."

"He tried to kill me!" Vanessa shrieked. She kept screaming it over and over until Anita and the young Mountie led her out. I had written the phrase 'witless with fear' several times; I had never seen it before.

"Anita?" Bernie repeated.

"Stay with Elizabeth," she ordered.

"Dave," called Hunter, "stay with Miss Mangold until I can get with you. Don't leave her alone."

A fierce look, half mutinous and half desperate, flashed over Officer Walters' face, but he manfully struggled with Vanessa's near dead weight. In a moment the door to Vanessa's room closed. Though muffled, we could still hear her screaming.

"What's going on? Liz, are you all right?" Bernie ran across the room to grab my hand. He hadn't changed into his dinner clothes yet. A slight stubble of beard shadowed his chin.

"Where have you been, Mr. Wingate?"

"Downstairs in the war room with Gilda Wilcox.

What's happened here? Liz..."

"May I speak to you a moment outside, Mr. Wingate?" Sergeant Hunter had politely phrased it as a question, but he was issuing an order and Bernie recognized it as such. Reluctantly, he released my hand and followed the sergeant into the hallway. They stood barely beyond the open door.

"Poor Vanessa," I murmured. "She's really frightened."

"So should you be," was Jared's succinct rejoinder. He stroked my hair tenderly, gently and then caressed my cheek. He had used to touch me like that, long ago. After a moment he asked in a tight voice, "Why did you go out, Lillybet? There's a murderer around here."

"I thought it was you."

"Why? Did he use my name? Did you hear his voice?"

"No...I had just called down to the bar, and you weren't there, and it was time for you to be here, and you've always had such a thing about being prompt..." It sounded lame, even to me. In some cases the truth can sound like a lie, whether you intend it to or not.

"And you just walked outside without asking who it was or anything. Honestly, Elizabeth..."

Now that sounded like the Jared I remembered.

"Yes, Miss MacAllister, why don't you tell us about it?" Sergeant Hunter, followed by Bernie, was now standing at the foot of my bed, his gaze locked with mine. I felt like a rabbit helpless before a wolf.

"I have."

"Pete..."

"Shut up, Jerry. I'm waiting, Miss MacAllister."

It was a most uncomfortable moment, made more so by Bernie's having turned to flip through the stuff I had left on the dresser. At the Mountie's tone, though, he turned around, his eyes glaring. "Just what are you insinuating, Sergeant?"

Hunter ignored him. "Why aren't you dead, Miss MacAllister?"

My mouth opened and closed fish-like a time or two before I could speak. It was true, and on some level I had realized it all along, but to have it put so baldly...I had to swallow twice before my voice would work. "I haven't the foggiest notion."

"Come on, Pete, she's had a rough time..."

"Not as rough as Jane Hall and Clement Wallingford. I want to know what made her immune."

Immune? He made murder sound like some sort of disease.

"We aren't even sure if it was the murderer who struck her..." Bernie said slowly.

"That's right, Pete. It could have been a sneak thief or something like that."

"You're both reaching."

"Well, it's not so crazy, is it? She's still alive..." Jared's strong pianist's fingers closed reassuringly on my shoulder.

"Please," I said meekly. "You're all shouting..."

Jared brushed a gentle hand over my hair. "Sorry, darling," he said, but the endearment was casual, the way entertainers say it a thousand times a day. "Look, maybe it was just some sort of crackpot..."

"Would you bet her life on that theory?"

There was a moment of silence, and then Jared protectively put his arm around me. "No."

"You aren't thinking of using Liz as some sort of lure, are you? I won't allow..." Bernie roared.

"We're just talking, Mr. Wingate." The sergeant was getting exasperated.

"Bernie, why don't you sit down?" I wanted him away from the dresser. He'd be dreadfully upset if I were working on the wrong book, especially since after all this he'd probably want *Daughters of Passion* sooner than before.

"I'm all right, Liz. Don't worry about me."

"We're still at the same question, Miss MacAllister." Now the sergeant's voice held something of an edge. "If we assume that the assailant was the killer, why didn't he kill you?"

I thought a moment. "Someone saw him?"

"And didn't raise an alarm?"

"Not enough time?"

"Our killer is a pro, Miss MacAllister."

Bernie goggled. "You mean a hit man? A professional killer?"

"Perhaps. He has enough knowledge of physiology to know where one quick thrust will kill. He's daring, and he's ruthless, and he's fast. It probably took less time to kill the other two than to knock you out."

* * *

After that, there was nothing I could say. I thought about lying here snugly cradled against Jared's chest—alive, feeling, thinking, knowing, breathing, blood pumping—instead of being something still and cooling under a stained blanket. The thought should have made me feel good, but somehow, it just made me feel frightened, somehow, terrified that life was so tenuous. I wanted to be alone, to think...

The door flashed open and closed just as quickly, and I only jumped about half a foot before seeing that it was Anita.

"I got Vanessa to take two Valiums," she said briskly and without preamble. "They should start taking effect soon. She's still upset, but the other policeman is with her. I didn't dare stay away any longer."

That was a strange remark, I thought, but somehow, it would take too much energy to question it. Jared wasn't as lazy, though, for he asked, "You didn't dare...?"

Her patrician gaze would have done justice to the most disdainful of queens. "Officer..."

"Sergeant, Ma'am." Hunter gritted his teeth.

"Very well, then, Sergeant, you trust this man. I do not."

Had she thrown a spitting cat into the middle of the bed I couldn't have been more surprised. Jared was many things, but try as I would, I couldn't picture him as a murderer.

"Anita!" Bernie spluttered.

"Would you explain that, please, Mrs. Wingate?"

Gracefully, Anita perched on the side of the bed and took my hand. It was a very pretty gesture, but as it was only a single bed, we were all very crowded. Besides, I had just gotten accustomed to my posture. Anita's weight, though slight, changed the position of the bed and set my head to throbbing wildly again.

"Certainly." Her eyes glittered. "I told you that last night, when I left Jane on this floor and went back down in the elevator, I saw a tall pale man in the hallway. At first, I thought it might be Clement...it was near his room, but then, after Jane was killed I started to think, and now that Clement is dead..."

Then Jared lost his temper. It is a popular belief that concert musicians have hair-trigger tempers and yell a lot. In Jared's case that was only half true. He did have a legendary hair-trigger temper, but he never shouted. Instead, his eyes would narrow to slits, and he would speak in a deep, slow, intensely controlled voice that raised the hair on the back of your neck. It doesn't sound too frightening to describe, but I have seen conductors hardened to every stunt a concert artist can pull blanch and give over when confronted with it.

Jared used it now, and the effect in the small room was electrifying. "You mean you think it was I?"

Even Anita wavered, but she held her ground; so far she was doing better than any symphony conductor I had ever seen.

"I saw a tall, pale man just before Jane was killed. Tonight, when I came out of my room to look for Bernard, I saw Elizabeth lying unconscious on the floor, and you bending over her. Heaven only knows what might have happened had I come out a minute later."

Jared leaned over me until he was almost nose-to-nose with Anita. His voice dropped another whole tone into the danger zone. "You think I would hurt

Elizabeth?"

"You were bending over her."

Sergeant Hunter's voice sounded like it came from another world. "What were you doing coming out of your room, Mrs. Wingate?"

"It was getting late. I wanted to see if I could be of help to Bernard."

"And you weren't scared, with a murderer loose?"

The Sergeant's voice had dripped with sarcasm, but Anita stared right back at him without wavering. "I am not a writer, Officer Hunter. What could anyone possibly have against me?"

He didn't even bother to correct her. "Okay, Jerry, why don't you tell us what happened?"

Slowly, like air leaking out of a balloon, the dreadful tension in the room began to dissipate.

"I told Elizabeth and the others that I would come back in twenty minutes to take them downstairs; you had told them to wait in their rooms — remember? — Which it seems Mrs. Wingate disregarded."

"I remember."

"I had to speak to Finlay, just as I was coming up. That made me about three or four minutes late. When I stepped out of the elevator I saw Elizabeth lying there on the floor. For a minute..." His voice faltered and stopped. He licked his lips and then took a deep breath. "When I got to her, I saw that she was still alive. I was trying to see if she was hurt when all of a sudden Mrs. Wingate started shrieking like a Valkyrie and calling for that Mangold woman to call you."

"And you didn't see anyone else in the hall?"

"No, not until after Mrs. Wingate started screaming. All I could see was Elizabeth lying there."

"And from there you can see the entire hall, and the lights aren't that dim," Hunter muttered angrily. "There's really no way anyone could hide there. Mrs. Wingate, did you see anyone else?"

"No. As I have told you, I stepped out of my door, saw this man hovering over Elizabeth and started screaming for help."

"Miss Mangold said that she heard knocking on her door just about the time you were supposed to be here, Jerry."

"Why didn't she open her door?"

"She said she was putting on her make-up. Miss Mangold admitted she heard the knocking, Mrs. Wingate." Frowning, Hunter muttered more to himself than to us, "So, if Miss MacAllister came out when she heard the knock, she could have lain there between two and four minutes."

"That means you were in danger of being killed for..." Bernie gasped. His solicitude would have been much more touching had I been sure it had been for me personally instead of for the best-selling author of *Sisters of Desire* and hopefully, others. Perhaps that was a harsh judgment, but nearly being killed has a strange effect on your mind.

"Why did you open the door without verifying who was there, Miss MacAllister?"

I shrugged. It hurt. "It had been twenty minutes. Jared has always been so very prompt..."

"Except this time," Anita said accusingly.

"Except this time." Jared's tone was equally venomous.

"And because of it Elizabeth was nearly killed."

"Please!" I cried. Maybe what they were saying was true, but neither the words nor their voices were comforting.

But had I nearly been killed? If the others had been dispatched so quickly and easily, why had I been allowed to lie there unmolested save for a lump on the head for over two minutes?

Had someone else come into the hallway and stopped the impending crime? If that were so, why didn't they raise an alarm or call for the Mounties? I sighed and gave up the effort. Thinking only made my head hurt worse.

"We're tiring you, Elizabeth," Anita said in quick perception. "You should rest. I'll stay with you."

Beneath me I could feel Jared's muscles tensing, and I couldn't stand another flare-up between the two of them; neither did I think I could take a whole night of Anita, solicitous or not.

"There's no need, Anita. I'm feeling much better."

"Are you sure, Lillybet?" Jared whispered. "You don't look at all well."

"Sorry, sweet thing," I answered with a nauseating flippancy. "I'm getting older; this is as good as it gets."

Bernie's face cleared. "That's our Liz. Game to the end."

"Well, Bernie, this is pretty close to it. I wish you all would get out of here and let me put my poor old aching bones to bed." I glanced around at them, trying not to look speculative, trying to see if my ploy worked.

"Actually, Miss MacAllister," the sergeant said, "the medicos tell us you shouldn't go to sleep after being hit on the head."

"All right," I answered, trying to keep my voice light. "I'm not sleepy anyway. I'll just read for a while."

"I do not want you left alone, Elizabeth..." Anita began, but Bernie interrupted her.

"Liz, are you sure you're all right?"

I smiled. "Yes, Bernie. You can go down to your dinner, if you like. Aside from a headache, which I intend to doctor with aspirin, I feel fine. Did you get hold of the Peters and Worcester people?"

"Gilda Wilcox said she'd call them. I've got to get changed. Everyone will be waiting..."

"Bernard! You can't seriously be thinking..."

I pressed my advantage. Everyone seemed to be growing roots. If I wanted to be left alone, I'd have to work at it. "Bernie, you have to..."

"Elizabeth!" Anita snapped. Her face was a study in frustration.

"Look...like the sergeant said, we've got to avoid a panic," I said, thinking fast, "and if that vampire reporter gets wind that something is wrong..."

"You don't have to work so hard to get us to go," Jared murmured.

Curse the man... How could he always read my mind exactly when I didn't want him to?

"The idea is patently ridiculous, Elizabeth," Anita pronounced. "How will we ever explain if none of 'The Fabulous Four' are there? Don't be ridiculous. The thing will just have to be canceled. Besides, you need care."

Sergeant Hunter was giving me a very strange look. "And you should be checked on periodically, Miss MacAllister. A head injury is nothing to be taken lightly."

Apparently being knocked on the head gives you a criminal mentality; at least, I hope so, because I'd hate to think I was so devious normally.

"My head is fine, sergeant. As for the dinner, Bernie, it couldn't be better...Tell them that you wanted to talk to them without any of us around. Hint that they might make us jealous..."

It was weak, but Bernie, grasping at straws, bought it. Anita took a little more persuading — it seemed as if she were bound and determined to play nursemaid to me — but finally Bernie's and my urging convinced her. Jared even swore he'd call up from the bar every half hour to check on me, which almost made Anita change her mind. It took a lot of talking and a great deal of rather good acting to make them think I felt a lot better than I really did. Anita still promised she'd check on me later.

I thought I had gotten away with it. I really thought he hadn't noticed, but as he turned to go Bernie picked up the notebook. He smiled indulgently as he read the label.

"*A Man of Honor?* Liz, what are you doing wasting your time working on this old war horse again? You should be finishing up *Daughters of Passion*. I'm going to be expecting a lot more out of you now..."

And he dropped it neatly in the wastebasket.

"Well, if you're going, you don't want to be late..." Sergeant Hunter said abruptly and all but hustled them out the door.

"Pete, I don't think it's wise for her to be here alone..."

"Jared, I was at his mercy out there...If the murderer didn't kill me when I was lying unconscious out in the hall, I don't think he's going to break through a locked door and kill me while I sleep."

"She's right, Jerry. I don't think the killer wants her. I just don't know why." Sergeant Hunter's gaze all but stripped my soul naked. I had to look away.

"I don't know either," I cried. "I'd tell you if I knew."

"You're upset," Jared said softly and reached to embrace me. "You shouldn't be left alone."

I dodged away. I shouldn't have, he was only trying to be kind, and besides, it made my head scream. I had just had enough of people telling me how I felt and how I should behave.

I looked him coldly in the eye. "You should have thought of that two and a half years ago!"

* * *

It had been a cruel and hard and unforgivable thing to say, a scorned woman's fantasy of revenge come true, and as soon as the words were spoken I wished that I could call them back...but they worked. I was alone in my room within twenty seconds.

Probably, it was all for the best. Probably. I kept repeating that word to myself as I gulped a couple of aspirins and splashed my face with cold water. I had to think, and a lot of emotion cluttering up the place would do no good. It dismayed me to find out just how much Jared could still affect me even now. Dragging up old dead feelings, saying things two and a half years dead never did anybody any good.

Ruthlessly, I shut all thoughts of Jared out of my mind. He was just one more problem, and I had enough to think about. Drying my face, I reached around for the zipper of my shiny silver dress, and then stopped. Poor dress, hardly an auspicious debut. Nobody had even noticed it.

I left the zipper alone. No matter what had happened, it was still beautiful, and I wanted to enjoy it just a little longer, even if I had to do it by myself. Turning on the old fashioned floor lamp, I draped the fur jacket around me, made myself comfortable in the armchair and started to think.

Some people have an image of writers as completely scatty-boo creatures, living without rules in a world of the imagination and having no grounding in real life. Maybe some are in some areas, but whether they show it or not, writers have to have a finely tuned sense of logic. To create a complicated and coherent story calls for a mind that can keep many strands of thought going at the same time and tie them all off neatly at the end. My editor told me that I have too much of that tendency, wanting to tell what happened to every character who was mentioned more than once. Perhaps it was a problem to them; it certainly was a problem to me now. I liked everything explained, all neat and tidy, with no loose strings.

All I had now was loose strings.

I sat and thought and thought and still nothing made sense.

Jane was dead.

Clement was dead.

I could have been dead, but I had been spared.

Why?

It was at times like this, worrying over a knotty problem that I almost wished I smoked. It must be very soothing to have something to do with the hands when you're thinking. There has to be some reason academics constantly fiddle with pipes. For lack of something else I absently began to finger the shiny paillettes that edged the seam of my gown.

I was alive.

Why?

We were all authors.

We all worked for Wingate Publications, now Wingate Romances.

The others had sold much more than I. Jane had published well over a hundred novels and Clement perhaps half that many, while I had sold only two, just one of which had been a romance. Vanessa had over thirty love stories to her credit, so perhaps she had been right in her claim that she was to have been the victim.

Was that why I had been ignored? I didn't have enough sales? Or was the killer going in order, and I was being saved until Vanessa had been taken care of, like some particularly toothsome morsel saved for dessert?

That was depressing.

I tried another line of thought.

Jared had seen no one when he found me unconscious; Anita had seen only him. I could not believe that either of them would lie, but neither could I believe that Jared was either the killer or the one who struck me. I had no logical proof of that, but I knew in my bones that Jared was no killer.

Neither would Anita lie. She might be snobbish, insufferably proud and a royal bitch at times, but I couldn't see her telling a deliberate lie. Her pride wouldn't let her.

So...where did that get me?

Nowhere.

Somebody had knocked on Vanessa's door. Both she and I had heard that.

Presumably, that same somebody had knocked me over the head.

Also, presumably, that same somebody had the ability to turn himself invisible, since no one had seen or heard his departure and no one had remained...

Or had they?

I sat forward, shocked into a painful state of awareness. Not only had one of the shiny silver paillettes come off in my hand—which left an ugly spot on the gown that would probably cost the earth to fix—my brain had finally snapped into gear. I had at least part of what was bothering me so.

Everyone talked about what they had seen and heard in the hallway, but everyone's attention had been on me. No one had made a search.

Arrogantly assuming that my immunity to violent death would last and buoyed up by my grand new idea, I tossed away the chipped and bent paillette and headed for the door. Slipping back the chain quietly, I braced myself against the door in case I should have to slam it shut again quickly and peeked up and down the empty hall, shivering in the chill air.

At first glance it was very depressing. This end of the hallway was about as simple as a hall could be. There was a long straight shot from the elevator, dead-ending in Bernie and Anita's suite. A small cul-de-sac served the three rooms of the battlement tower and every inch of it was visible from the elevator area.

There was no way that anything bigger than a mouse could have hovered in the shadows and then made their escape while Jared was occupied with me. The lights were purposefully dimmed because of the power emergency, but even so, there weren't any shadows, and Vanessa's room, being closest to the elevators, was the most brightly lit of all.

I said a most unladylike word, and ready to concede defeat, started to close the door. But...

My brain must still have been working in high gear, for I saw, actually saw, what had been before me since I had arrived.

Just a little way down the hall, almost opposite Vanessa's door, was another door. It wasn't a room door, or even a proper door. Half the width of a regular door, it had no numbers, and instead of being dark brown like the room doors, it was papered to look like part of the wall.

I made another quick check up and down the hall, and then tiptoed shiveringly across. Don't ask why I tiptoed when there was no one in sight; it just seemed a time for silence. You never know what you're going to disturb with a lot of noise.

The little door swung open at a light touch. Beyond, in a space barely larger than a dining table, were a washer and dryer. Coin operated. This was a self-laundry provided for the hotel guests.

And, this could have been where my attacker had gone. It was only a step or two from where I had lain. The murderer had simply stepped in there, waited until the furor was over, then either disappeared or joined the crowd.

But *why* hadn't he killed me?

It was cold in the dismal little room, and I shivered. I still didn't have enough information, but maybe this would twig something in either Anita's or Jared's mind. Maybe they saw something but dismissed it as unimportant. Going back to my room, I took two more aspirins and grabbed my coat.

For whatever reason, the murderer had spared me. That didn't mean I would offer the same courtesy.

Chapter Nine

"Elizabeth!" Anita spluttered. She looked up from a barely touched plate of Chicken Divan. The heavenly smell made me realize I was hungry, but I didn't have time to worry about food now.

"Liz!" Bernie jumped to his feet.

There were about a dozen eager faces there, some in full evening dress, some in more casual things. One rather androgynous looking creature was recognizable as female just because she was wearing a dress, a spectacular creation of pink tulle and ribbon roses that made my silver spangles seem conservative.

"What are you doing down here?"

"Anita, I knew we agreed tonight was going to be just for Bernie's new discoveries," I said quickly, making a game effort to stick to our story.

"You didn't come down here by yourself..." Bernie hissed.

"Of course I did," I answered brightly and grabbed Anita's arm, making her come with me. "I hate to disturb you all, but I just need to talk to Anita for one little minute."

When we were safely out of sight Anita grabbed my arm with surprising strength. Her face was taut with fear. "Elizabeth, what is all this about? You should be in bed."

"I'm all right..."

"And did you forget that there is a murderer in this hotel? I thought you were going to stay safely in your room. How did you get down here?"

It had been easy. I had merely stepped out of my room, rung for the elevator and ridden it down to the first floor. Of course, it hadn't been that simple, especially not on my nerves. I had started at every whisper of sound, looked fearfully into every shadow, listened to my heart thudding louder and louder.

"It wasn't that bad," I muttered. "Anita..."

She was still upset. "But were you not terrified? Elizabeth, there is a murderer loose in this hotel."

"He could have killed me a dozen times over while I was unconscious. I don't know why, but I don't think he wants to harm me."

"Yet."

She could have talked all evening without saying that.

Suddenly the lights flickered and then failed altogether. The small decorative candles on each table seemed to emphasize the sudden darkness rather than relieve it. Outside the big arched windows there was a pale glow, as if the snow had a power source of its own. You could almost hear the entire hotel holding its breath until a moment later when everything blinked back on, though not as brightly.

"Looks like the generator repairs weren't as successful as they thought," Anita said. Her voice held a frightened edge. "Elizabeth, please let us take you back to your room..."

"No, just listen to me. We mustn't stay too long, or the new writers will start to wonder. When you saw me lying in the floor and Jared holding me..."

"Bending over you."

"Whatever. You said there was no one else in the hall..."

"Elizabeth, I know that man was once your husband, and you probably still have some residual feelings for him, but I don't trust him."

"Anita, please! Can you just answer my question?"

"No, there was no one else in the hall. Now, will you let me take you back up to your room where you'll be safe?"

"I can't go now," I said and watched her face go from urgency to real fear. I couldn't blame her; inside I was all quivering jelly. "Do you remember that little door across the hall from mine?"

She looked as if I had lost my mind. It did sound like a *non sequitur*, even to me, so I repeated the question.

"Door? I don't remember a door there. Elizabeth, what are you talking about? Maybe you were hit harder than we thought..."

I dodged her almost maternal caress. "There's a tiny door that leads to a laundry room. It isn't locked. There's a possibility that whoever hit me could have hidden in there when he heard the elevator coming, so when you opened your door you saw only Jared."

"Do you really think so?" she asked in strained tones. Perhaps she was just now realizing how closely she had come to walking into the murderer.

"It's the only possibility. I know you don't like Jared," I said quickly, forestalling the reply that visibly leapt to her lips, "and he does have his problems, but I can't picture him as a killer, any more than I can you or

Bernie."

Her expression softened. "Do you really trust him so much?"

"Anita, think about it. If Jared were going to kill me he would have done it long ago. And, what could he possibly have against Jane or Clement?"

"Well, if that's how you feel..." Her hand gripped mine tightly. "I'm still worried about you. You can't be sure the killer won't hurt you the next time. You have too much talent to risk."

"I know, but...I didn't mean it that way. I know the killer could change his mind, but I've got to do what I can. Now, run back to your dinner. I've got to talk to Jared and find out if he saw anything."

It took a little more convincing to dissuade her from calling the Mounties to escort me back to my room right there and then, but finally she went back into the dining room, a worried look on her face.

"Be careful," was her parting warning. "That horrible reporter is lurking around looking for someone on whom she can pounce. She practically forced herself into our party, and we had to have her ejected from the dining room."

Great, just great!

Frankly, I was worried too, and not just about a scavenging reporter; after our acrimonious parting Jared might not want to talk to me. Still, I had to try.

From the dining room I walked past the game room, the big double doors not quite masking the irritating beeps and buzzes and dings of the machines. To the right was the deserted elegance of the writing room, to the left the elevator bank and in the center the grand stairway down to the ground floor. There was no one on the broad, straight, magnificent staircase.

I couldn't resist it. I floated down the stairs in the best tradition of romantic heroines. In the happy times, before everything had become a life or death affair, I had toyed with a hazy idea of setting some sort of novel here and having my heroine sweeping down these stairs to meet her lover.

Of course, no one noticed my descent. The lobby was fairly full, as if no one wanted to endure the isolation of their rooms. Ralph Harcourt was holding forth in one corner, a group of wide-eyed conferees regarding him raptly. He nodded and waved as I went past. A well-known agent, more known for her unusual sexual proclivities than for her skills as a salesperson, was talking earnestly to a pretty young woman, and I wondered which side of her nature she was pushing. Next to the windows, a couple of assistant editors from some of the smaller publishing houses were holding an impromptu panel session, answering questions and giving their house's policies.

Behind them the windows stood like great dark eyes. The outside spotlights had been turned off, probably to spare the generator; if the snow were still falling the way it had all day, they would be useless anyway. Just beyond the glass there was the ghost of motion, as the inside lights picked up a few drifting flakes. It gave a strange impression of movement, as if we were under water.

The bar was crowded, but even over the continuous

rumble of conversation I could hear Jared's playing. Right now it was a heavy-handed version of a sugary Stephen Foster medley.

Poor Jared. He hated Stephen Foster only slightly less than Rodgers and Hammerstein, and his playing showed it. It never ceased to amaze me that he possessed such artistry as to make every note of Chopin or Liszt or Debussy or Beethoven or a dozen others sing with emotion and clarity, and yet he could still make such a feelingless hash of the more popular composers whom he disliked.

For a moment I stood in the door of the bar and watched him. He was frowning and banging away at the piano like a bad second-year student. There was no cluster of adoring fans around him now; probably no one dared brave that dark scowl.

Well, I didn't particularly want to either, but there wasn't any choice. I had to talk to him about that door...and to apologize. After that I didn't ever have to speak to him again.

Did I want to?

"Miss MacAllister?"

"Go away, Miss Huggins."

Eyes bright as a squirrel's, Taylor Huggins planted herself directly in front of me. She had changed from her ski outfit into a long dark skirt, a vibrant red turtleneck and a gaudy multicolor vest—sort of 'Barbie™ Après Ski.'

"Don't be like that, Miss MacAllister...I just want to ask a few questions about Wingate Romances and its writers..."

"No comment."

She gave a deep, exasperated sigh. "Very well, if you're going to be that way...Are the rumors of your being attacked true?"

I tried to step around her. She stepped right in front of me again. We repeated the exercise. She could have a great future as a cutting horse.

"You are annoying me. Please go away."

"Now if you'll just answer a few questions..."

"No." I gave her a glare fully equal to any of Anita's. During the short time after Jared's accident when the press had been trying to get my part of the story that glare had protected me. It didn't even dent the hunger in her eyes.

"But I'm the press, Miss MacAllister. The public has a right to know what's going on here."

I itched to slap that smug, perky face. Instead my fingers closed tightly over the hard metal shell of the new silver evening bag. "The public's right to know ends where my right to privacy begins. I have nothing to say to you."

"Are you trying to protect the man who attacked you?"

We were attracting attention. Ripples of curious looks flowed toward us like waves of cloyingly warm air. Straightening my posture, I spoke a bit louder than necessary.

"Miss Huggins, if you do not go away and leave me alone I shall have you forcibly removed by hotel security."

The bright *façade* cracked, showing an odd mixture of anger and embarrassment beneath. "That's not fair," she snarled. "I'm a reporter."

"There is a big difference between reporting and vulgar curiosity," I said shortly. "Will you please let me pass?"

The glare she gave me would have melted steel, but she stepped aside, and as I passed, whispered an epithet that Barbie™ would never have admitted knowing.

Putting on a brave smile and trying to ignore the faint but persistent throbbing in my head, I threaded my way through the crowded room. As in most bars, the tables were tiny, but here instead of plain chairs they had great-upholstered easy ones and when six or eight were pulled up around a table only slightly bigger than the average pizza it made crossing the room quite a proposition. I didn't envy the waitresses.

"Miss Allison..." began a heavyset matron in an exquisitely cut purple suit. She struggled out of the chair with an effort. "I'd like to ask..."

I evaded her outreaching hand without even slowing down.

"Well!" she sniffed in injured hauteur. "You don't have to be so snooty." Then to her friends, "Aren't they supposed to be here to help us get published?"

Another fan lost. At the moment I didn't care. There were other things that were much more important.

"Jared..."

He didn't even look up. "Go away, Elizabeth. We don't have anything to say to each other."

"Darn it, listen to me!" I hissed, leaning over the piano. "I came down here to apologize."

Unfortunately, it sounded more like a threat. He

glanced up expressionlessly and then looked back down at the keys. From Foster he slid down a showy glissando into "The Impossible Dream", which I thought unnecessarily ironic. Aside from that, every note felt like a little hammer inside my brain; the aspirin had been useless.

I took a deep breath and started again. "Look, Jared, I don't know why I was such a bitch earlier. All I can say is that I was hit over the head, I'm scared out of my wits, and I'm sorry. It was a stupid, cruel thing to say. I thought I had all that out of my system a long time ago."

He thundered into "As Time Goes By" and promptly missed three major chords. I had forgotten how magically he moved over the keys, the way his fingers curved and flashed, the play of muscles over the backs of his hands...Somehow that touched me more than anything else which had happened between us this weekend. When we were newly married I had sat and watched him practice by the hour. It was then that my mind had started to create *A Woman of Quality*.

As if to erase his mistake, he ran a great showy arpeggio the length of the keyboard and back, then began to play a simple old tune called "To A Wild Rose". It almost broke my heart. That was his signature tune, the one he had always used as a final encore to show that the performance was irrevocably over.

"And you do now?"

"I guess so."

He was silent a moment, and when he spoke again his voice had a flat, detached quality. "What are you doing down here? You were supposed to stay put."

"I wanted to apologize, and I wanted to ask you a question."

He glanced upward, and there was a flash of curiosity the depths of his dark eyes. "A question?"

"You said, tonight that when you found me, there wasn't anyone else in the hall."

"That's right."

"Did you happen to notice a small door just across from my room?"

"A door?" He gave me the same sort of look Anita had, as if he too doubted my sanity. "No, I just saw you. What's this about a door?"

"It's a little laundry room...I was just wondering if whoever hit me might have stepped in there when he heard the elevator coming..."

His scowl returned, but now it was with thought instead of hostility. "That's reaching, Elizabeth."

"I know, but it takes the suspicion off you and Anita." The woman just behind me had ordered a miniature quiche, and the smell was fantastic. I couldn't decide which was stronger, my headache or my hunger. It was a struggle to come back to business. "Did you see anything else, anything at all, even if it doesn't seem important?"

He wasn't thinking of his playing. "To A Wild Rose" was over, and his fingers had slipped automatically into one of Chopin's gentler waltzes. The notes poured into the air like warm honey.

"No..." he said after a moment. "Like I told you, when the elevator doors opened all I could see was you lying there on the floor. That silver thing is hard to miss. I ran over to you, saw you were still breathing then lifted your shoulders to see if there was any sort of a wound. I didn't see any blood, and then the next thing I knew, that Wingate woman was standing behind me, screeching her lungs out." He made an expression of distaste. Jared had never liked loud noises unless he made them. "Then Pete and Dave showed up, and you finally started to come around."

I gnawed my lower lip. "Then you took me into my room and everyone followed. If somebody had been hiding in that laundry room, they could have strolled right out without anybody seeing them. And it still doesn't answer why I wasn't killed like the others." I rubbed my temples. This was like one of those horrible mazes when every time you go down a corridor it turns into a blind alley.

"Have you told the Mounties about this?"

"No, just you and Anita. Guess I better talk to them, though. Where are they?"

"Probably up in the Cariboo Suite. They've been using it for a command center."

"On the third floor?"

"Yes..." He looked up suddenly. "You aren't running around by yourself, are you?"

"He didn't hurt me, Jared."

He brought his hands down on the keys in a crashing discord, and for a moment, all conversation in the bar ceased as quickly as if cut off by a knife. Standing, Jared glared at the crowd, and as a wave of slightly embarrassed babble washed around us, grabbed my arm.

"You little fool," he growled as he half-dragged me

from the crowded bar. "Don't you realize you could be killed? Death is so damned permanent…"

His face was rigid. He had to be thinking of Jennifer. Was he still in love with her? A pang went through me, and I tried to believe that it was only sympathy for him. At least with the loved one still alive there was always a hope, however slim, for reconciliation, but as he said, death was indeed permanent. I shuddered.

"Are you all right?"

His gaze was so penetrating; I feared it would reveal my innermost thoughts, thoughts I couldn't even admit to myself. I looked away and said the first thing that came into my mind. "I'm hungry."

"Hungry? Have you eaten today?"

I thought back. It had been such a long, eventful day, and in the grand scheme of things food hadn't seemed very important. "Just a Danish this morning and a couple of those little tea sandwiches."

"Dieting?"

"No."

"You just like starving yourself, I suppose." He jabbed the elevator button savagely.

"I didn't think about it," I answered defensively.

"I'll get you something while you're talking to Pete."

"Do you think the alleged attack on your ex-wife is tied in with the Wingate murders?"

Taylor Huggins popped up as suddenly—and as welcome—as a toadstool. She gave me a cold glare of triumph and then turned a dazzling smile on Jared.

Obviously, she had no knowledge of his opinions regarding intrusive reporters. I could almost—almost! —

feel sorry for her as I automatically took a step back out of the danger zone.

"Murders?" Jared gave her a smile fully as toothy and false as her own. "What murders?"

"Why, Jane Hall and... and...You can't keep things from the press forever."

"I suggest you lie down for a while," Jared said with poisonous solicitude. "Or talk to the Mounties. I'm sure they'll give you whatever information you desire."

"But they wouldn't..." Something very ugly passed over Taylor's perfect face as she caught herself. She was resilient and persistent; without pausing for breath she took another tack. "Was your meeting here planned or an accident?"

Jared glared at her.

"Are you planning to get back together?"

I glared at her.

"You were playing something classical a moment ago...Does this mean you're planning a return to the concert stage?"

Jared began to tick. It wasn't audible, of course, but the fuse on his temper had just been lit. I stepped even further out of the danger zone and jabbed wildly at the elevator button again just as the doors opened.

"I will tell you this only once, so you had better listen," Jared said in his lowest, softest, most dangerous voice. "Keep out of my business, or I will personally wring your nosy neck!"

* * *

The law was no more pleased with my exploring than Anita and Jared had been. His eyes cold, Pete

Hunter listened to my tale with stone-faced stolidity. I had always felt that he didn't like me, that he didn't believe me, and now, it was more obvious than ever. It was a distressing feeling. I finished my story, stammering at little at the last then sat in uncomfortable silence. Given a choice, I would rather have talked to the more sympathetic Officer Walters, but he wasn't there.

After a nerve-wrenching length of time Sergeant Hunter finally spoke. "Is that all, Miss MacAllister?"

"What do you mean, 'all'?"

"Surely that isn't enough information to risk your life for."

"I don't understand."

"What do you mean, Pete?"

The policeman regarded Jared with an almost pitying look. "She's such a heroine...risking her life to question you and Mrs. Wingate. God save me from amateur detectives...if that's the real reason."

"Just what is that supposed to mean?" Jared's voice dropped a whole tone.

I forced my back erect and tried not to think about my aching head. The most painful throbbing had localized into a fist-sized area near the base of my skull. If I could only cut out that portion, I just might live.

"I mean that Miss MacAllister either thinks we're stupid or she's trying very hard for some attention."

Jared's face darkened dangerously. "Now look here..."

"No, you look here! Don't play the outraged and protective lover, Jerry. I think that's just what she wants. Do you really think we would be stupid enough to ignore something as obvious as a door?"

No. Of course they wouldn't, and if I had stopped to think for half a second, it would have been obvious. My ego said that the blow to my head had scrambled my thought processes, but my rational brain said nothing of the kind. I had simply been stupid, criminally stupid. A cop like Sergeant Pete Hunter would never have missed anything like that.

"And you found nothing."

"Right, Miss MacAllister. Nothing. And no one."

"When did you look?"

"Dave glanced in while everyone was trying to bring you around. As you know, there's not enough room in there for concealment if the door is opened. Then I checked it personally after I left your room. In fact, Dave is probably checking it again right now. I've got him on rounds."

"Rounds? What about Vanessa? And Anita and Bernie?"

He shrugged and smiled. "She is safe as long as she keeps her door locked. After all, there are only two of us."

"What about hotel security?"

Something very ugly entered his eyes. "They've got their hands full with other things. You seem very concerned about Miss Mangold's safety, Miss MacAllister."

"Someone should be," I answered as tartly as Anita at her worst. He was being very cavalier towards Vanessa's safety, but at the moment my own problems bothered me more. "And you didn't find anything in the laundry room?"

Without warning the room went dark. This time I was so overwrought I couldn't help a small squeal, an indication of weakness that was intensely embarrassing. Only the strong warmth of Jared's hand closing over mine kept the worst of my fears at bay. We waited a heart-stopping length of time before they flickered and came on again with a watery glow.

"That generator will never hold until morning," Sergeant Hunter said gloomily. "All we need is a blackout."

"The laundry room," Jared prompted. "There was nothing?"

"Both times."

"I didn't know," breathed Jared.

"We were going to have forensics out here to look over that little room once we could get them up here." Hunter's voice dripped sarcasm.

"Well, why didn't you lock the place, then?" I snapped, trying to hide my embarrassment in anger.

"And if the killer did hide in there..." his voice made this sound, an implausible possibility, "...he would know we suspected and destroy the place, along with any evidence that was there. Of course, we didn't count on our own home grown detective going in there and messing things up. Did you touch anything in there, Miss MacAllister?"

"Just the door...and the edge of the washer...I felt sick at heart. "My fingerprints must be all over the place."

"Exactly." He smiled tightly. It was a very ugly

expression.

Now my stomach knotted and throbbed almost as much as my head. He was all but accusing me of being the murderer.

"Two people have been killed," the sergeant was saying slowly. "You say you were only attacked. I think we can rule out the possibility that your 'attack' was not connected to the murders. Yet, after two murders and being attacked yourself, you go out all alone to investigate the evidence. I wouldn't believe that even in a TV movie, so, I have to wonder what your real purpose was."

"I told you everything I did from the time I left the room."

"I know you did, Miss MacAllister. I was following you every step of the way."

"What?"

"You really didn't think I'd just let you lock your door and ignore you, did you?" He smiled nastily. "You've been watched by hotel security ever since you stepped out of your room. They've told me every move you made by walkie-talkie."

"Then you can prove I'm telling the truth."

"I can prove what you want us to believe as truth."

"What do you mean by that?" Jared snapped. He clamped a hand on my shoulder; he wished only to be comforting, but he forgot how strong his fingers were. They hurt.

"I think I understand..." I said slowly. "You think I made the whole episode up. Next you'll say I did the murders."

Hunter nodded. "That's a pretty good theory, too. Both Hall and Wallingford were outselling you, getting more publicity, probably more money. You wanted to eliminate the competition."

"That's ridiculous," I spat. "I'm not even sure I want to go on writing romances, or writing period."

Jared's fingers began to knead my shoulder in unconscious agitation, and I squirmed until he quit. His voice dropped a whole tone more. "Dammit, Pete, you're going too far, and you know it."

"Not really." Hunter crossed his arms and leaned back against the desk. At that moment, I loathed the supercilious bastard. "You're her ex-husband. Maybe she wanted to get your attention, make you sorry for her, protective of her, maybe even get back together with you. Maybe she wanted publicity. Maybe..."

"I am not a murderer!"

"No, and apparently you are not a murderer's victim, either."

"So if I get killed, you'll admit I'm innocent?" The whole affair was taking on a nightmarish quality. My head beat like...like something horrible and heavy. I had run out of suitable similes.

"Pete, that's enough." Jared snapped.

"Think about it, Jerry. What better way to take the suspicion off her than to be attacked? Easy to accomplish by lying on the floor and pretending to be knocked out."

That did it. "Pretending?" I bellowed ignoring the painful echoes it set up in my head. "How do you suppose I got this knot on the back of my head?"

"Knot? Let me see, Elizabeth." Even though his

fingers were as conscientiously gentle as a surgeon's it hurt when Jared parted my hair. I couldn't help yelping.

"Careful! That's tender."

"I can see why, Lillybet. You have a real goose egg there. You should have let us send for a doctor earlier."

"I don't like doctors."

"I know that. Why didn't you say something about this before?"

"I was too busy being accused of murder," I snarled incautiously.

"It's been bleeding, too."

"And I suppose you think I did that myself, too?"

The sergeant shrugged. "It's possible. Plus, we have no proof you had that when you were lying in the hall."

"That's enough, Pete." Jared said quietly. "I mean it. Lillybet, have you put anything on this?"

I shook my head and regretted it. "Now, *Officer* Hunter," I said spitefully, "do you really think I could do that to myself? And with what?"

With a quickness that showed he had already considered that question, Sergeant Hunter picked up my silver shell evening bag and turned it over slowly.

"With this. It's metal, rigid enough for a blow and easy to clean."

Jared looked up, his face stormy and dark. "My God, Pete, look at her head. It's all bruised and cut. Do you think she hit herself that hard?"

"Small price to pay to exempt herself from suspicion of murder and get your attention again."

"You are sick…" I growled, though at that moment I felt almost capable of a murder—his. "Or…ambitious! It

198

would really look good for you to have this all solved by the time they dig us out of here, wouldn't it? Do you get extra points for arresting someone famous?"

The sudden coldness in his eyes confirmed that I had struck a nerve.

"Don't thrash around so much, Lillybet. You've made it bleed again. Do you want to see a doctor?"

"The hotel doctor left when the ski season ended," Sergeant Hunter said neutrally. "But there's a doctor with the conference. A Dr. Wilcox."

I remembered him vaguely, an older man with an unhealthy fondness for alcohol. "Gilda Wilcox's husband? He's a proctologist."

"He's still a physician, Lillybet."

"I don't want to see him!" Antipathy, both personal and professional, aside, by this time of night the chances of him being sober were practically microscopic.

"All right, all right, you don't have to see him if you don't want to. It doesn't look like it needs any stitches. Pete, do you have any antiseptic or some alcohol?"

For a minute it looked like he would say no, then Hunter's face relaxed. "There's some aftershave. I got it downstairs today."

"Okay, I guess it'll have to do," Jared answered hesitantly. When the sergeant returned with a gaudy bottle he regarded it with a critical eye. "At least it has a high alcohol percentage. I don't understand your attitude, Pete. How can you think Elizabeth is a suspect?"

"I suspect everyone."

"Maybe you'll get your own TV show."

"Don't be nasty, Miss MacAllister. I told you that

earlier."

"My head didn't hurt then. Yeow!" I screeched as Jared applied an aftershave soaked tissue to my head. "That hurts."

"It's good for you. Now be still."

"Jared..."

"You don't want an infection, do you? Sit still."

I gritted my teeth and sat still, even though it felt like he was applying liquid fire to my poor abused head. Finally, when the worst was over, when I had either gotten used to the pain or my nerve ends had been completely burned away, I looked up at Sergeant Hunter. He was still turning my evening bag idly over in his hands.

"Sergeant, I am not guilty. Who do you think is really the murderer?"

His face darkened, and he looked piercingly at me. "I don't know, Miss MacAllister, but I assure you I am going to find out."

* * *

"How's your head?" Jared asked.

"It still hurts, no thanks to you," I answered grumpily. "What on earth did you put on it?"

"It was called Alpine."

"It stinks."

"Sorry. There wasn't much choice."

We had left the Mounties' suite a few minutes before. There had been a tense moment when I feared the aptly named Hunter would arrest me and lock me into a room until the snow cleared enough for us to get to jail. After that, there had been a worse moment when I feared

Jared would do something violent and unforgivable, but I really hadn't needed to worry about that. He might not regard himself as the world's greatest concert pianist any more, but that didn't mean he would risk his hands by doing anything overtly physical.

Jared pushed the elevator button, then— surprisingly—draped his arm most companionably around my shoulders and pulled my head over to rest against his chest.

"Better?"

"Very pleasant, but the only thing that would make my head feel better now is if I could take it off and put it in the refrigerator overnight."

He chuckled. "Still hungry?"

"Starving. I could eat a horse."

"Sorry, I don't think they have that on the menu, but I'm sure they can find you some appropriate substitution. Elk, maybe, or perhaps a caribou..."

"Don't make me laugh, please...it hurts." Still, after the horrors of the day, the pain of even a forced chuckle was more than worth it. Turning my head slightly I looked up at him. It wasn't the best of angles, as nearly all I could see was his jaw and soaring cheekbone. He needed a shave, as he nearly always did any time after mid-afternoon.

That dark shadow of beard was the only thing familiar about him; Jared had never been so solicitous or thoughtful. Oh, he had spoiled me thoroughly in the early days of our marriage, but it had been a manifestation of his pleasures, not my wants. Perhaps it was indicative that I had developed an unflatteringly suspicious nature, but I wondered what he wanted. Jared could always be utterly charming when he wanted something.

"Come on, then," he said with a disarming grin. "Let's go a-hunting."

He didn't bother to remove his arm as we stepped into the elevator, but it didn't rate even a raised eyebrow from the elevator girl. Either everyone was used to the sight of Jared and me now or the shadow of murder had obscured such ordinary things as gossip.

Fat chance. When we stepped off into the lobby every eye swiveled to stare, and the crashing babble of conversation died away to a trickle. Even though Jared immediately released me, assuming a more conventional posture by putting his hand on my elbow, I could feel all the little romantic minds there clicking, filing away our romantic posture.

It's none of your business, I wanted to shout, but that would only have made things worse. I put on what we had always called my 'celebrity wife face'—a slight smile and a pleasant, if somewhat blank expression—and allowed him to lead me to a table.

"The kitchen's probably closed, but I'll go see if I can find someone to rustle up something."

Everyone's gaze followed him as he strode quickly away then swiveled back to me.

It was like sitting naked on the tundra. Would I be mobbed by unpublished writers, clamoring for me to help them get published? Right now I couldn't even help myself.

Nervously, I began to finger the silver paillettes on

the seam of my gown, then, remembering the ugly gap I had created earlier, made myself stop. No need to make it worse. Fixing it was going to cost enough as it was.

With the suddenness of a wave the conversation washed back, a little too brightly, a little too loud, a little too forced. Now everyone I could see was studiedly looking away, but even so, I still felt like a bug on a microscope. Now all that was needed to make it perfect would be for that idiot apprentice reporter to show up again.

The gods were with me, however, and the figure that materialized at my side was that of the waitress. I ordered a brandy. Even with my jacket on I still felt cold. A few sips should warm me, and Jared could have the rest when he came back.

By the time Jared returned a few minutes later. I had drunk it all and was considering ordering another in spite of—or perhaps because of—the slight fuzziness it created in my head.

"Come on," he said, unceremoniously hauling me to my suddenly unsteady feet.

"Come on where?" I asked, grabbing his arm for support. Suddenly all the eyes in the room were focused back on us.

"Are you all right?"

"Just a little dizzy...I had a brandy to warm me up. It's cold."

"Brandy? Good grief, woman, you never had a head for spirits even when you hadn't been bashed around. Don't you know you're not supposed to have alcohol when you have a head injury?"

"Aren't you?"

"Switched if I know," he answered with a sudden, disarming grin. "Sounds good. Seems like I heard it once."

He put a steadying arm around my waist. We must have looked like lovers as we walked to the elevators. Funny, we had never walked like that when we actually were lovers. Jared always had to be separate, himself, visible...

"Seventh floor, please."

The elevator girl looked startled. "But Mr. Grant, it's all shut up. There's nothing open up there."

"It's all right, Mattie. Finlay's okayed it. Take us on up."

At first glance the seventh floor looked just like every other upper floor, save that it was done in shades of red instead of yellow or orange. The hall lights were burning dimly and the chilly air was preternaturally still. The isolation, the desolation, was almost palpable. It was cooler here than downstairs, but not as uncomfortable as I had feared. Maybe the heat had been closed off on this floor, but enough had crept up to make it fairly bearable. I tugged my jacket zipper all the way up to my neck.

"Sorry it took so long, but I wanted this to be something special."

He was being charming again, which made me skeptical.

"That was kind of you," I said easily. "Elk or caribou?"

"Roast beef. Sandwiches. They were all I could scrounge. The kitchen was pretty hectic."

"Roast beef sounds great. Why are we up here, Jared?"

"It was too noisy and crowded downstairs. Finlay suggested we have our supper up here." His voice tightened. In the dim light I couldn't see his eyes. "I wanted to talk to you, Lillybet. Not about what's going on here...about us."

"A confession scene?" I asked with a false lightness, my heart plummeting. Yesterday (just *yesterday*?) I had wondered about Jennifer, why he had left me for her. Now I felt that was a Pandora's Box, better left closed.

"Sort of. Don't look so grim. I've tried to make it as pleasant as possible." He patted my shoulder then took my hand and led me around to the right, stopping in front of an enormous pair of double doors.

"Jared, what is this?"

He pulled out a key. "The new dining room. They named it after somebody or other, but everyone just calls it the new dining room. I know how badly you must be wanting to get out for a while, so maybe this will do."

Odd he should say that. I hadn't felt the least confined, at least not until he had mentioned it. The lock gave, and with a flourish, he threw both doors open onto a fairyland.

Three sides of the room were nothing but glass, floor to ceiling. It was almost like walking out onto a terrace. There were a number of tables, gaunt and naked looking without their cloths, and a long buffet down the center of the room, equally bare and a grand piano crouched in the corner, but I saw all those later.

It was the moon we saw first.

The snow had stopped, and as quickly as they had come, the stormy clouds were blowing away. Already they were nothing more than rags scattered across the sky, allowing the bloated and brilliant moon to play hide and seek over the ground. And the ground...

The snow lay thick and soft on the land, its sleek whiteness obliterating all but the mountains themselves. Even their harsh slopes were padded and softened with white. Under the glowing moon the snow sparkled and seemed to pulse with an odd bluish light of its own. The outside spotlights were still off, but the lights from inside the hotel spilled out unimpeded, making dirty yellow spots on the pristine blue-white snow.

"Jared, it's beautiful..."

"The snow's over," he said in an odd tone. "They should have us dug out of here by noon."

"Noon?" It was sort of a shock to think of the outside world intruding. I had sort of gotten used to the idea of this weird insularity going on and on and on. By this time tomorrow night I could probably be on a plane heading south.

If Sergeant Hunter didn't have me arrested for murder.

Jared chuckled. It sounded forced. "I just thought we could be alone up here and talk. I didn't know there was going to be such a spectacular view. Madam, your dinner."

One table had a cloth, table settings and a large covered tray. There was even a small posy of fresh carnations; they were almost visibly shivering. With a flourish worthy of the snootiest *maitre d'* Jared raised the dome-shaped cover. The smell of hot beef teased my nose.

"Jared, how sweet..."

He pulled out my chair, and after I was seated, sat opposite me then served us both. "You said you were hungry. And...I thought this might be a good place for us to talk."

I had taken a hungry bite out of my sandwich, but the returning rush of reality strangled my appetite. "What are we going to talk about?"

"There are things left unfinished between us, Elizabeth."

If I had wanted I could have become very nasty. I could have reminded him that it had been he who severed the relationship so quickly, that it had been he who decided to leave me, that...

Oh, what was the use?

Now remarkably unhungry, I forced myself to take another bite of sandwich, chew and swallow before answering. It was quite as good as counting to ten.

"Why, Jared?" I asked at last. "Are you trying to make me feel bad all over again or whitewash your conscience or what?"

He pushed his plate away. In the cold blue moonlight the hot sandwich steamed slightly. "None of those reasons, actually. I wanted to apologize."

Whatever I had expected, that wasn't it.

He went on, his eyes staring sightlessly out at the beauty below. "I was wrong to leave you like that. Maybe, I was wrong to leave you at all. Anyway, I'm sorry."

Jared Granville, gifted, arrogant, darling of the musical world, was apologizing? *Mirabile dictu!*

"Why have you given up your music?"

"You asked me that once before." At least he didn't waffle about playing piano for a living. For the Jared Granville I knew the ear candy he had been playing didn't even qualify as music.

"I know. Right after we found Jane. You said you'd lost it."

"I have." He spread his hands and looked at them as if they were strange artifacts of another culture. In the queer blue-white light they looked like dead things. "Good only for playing trash music to half-drunk barflies."

"Self-pity?" I asked sarcastically then caught myself. Old hates were the bitterest and the least productive. I didn't like this new side of my character. "Sorry. Maybe it was bad for both of us that we met here. An unlucky accident."

"It wasn't an accident. It was Fate."

"What?"

"I lied to you, Elizabeth. I followed your career. I was in the hospital for quite a while after the wreck and then convalescent..." He spoke simply, directly, without self-pity or emotionalism. "A few of our friends stayed in touch with me...They told me about your switching to romances. It's a shame."

"You knew? You came here deliberately?" Somewhere at the bottom of my breastbone there was a knot of pain that made my aching head pale in comparison. They couldn't dig me out of this snowbound hell fast enough. Did he think just because Jennifer was gone I'd be waiting to take him back like some sort of faithful understudy? Didn't he think I had any pride?

His next words were proof of the eerie sort of communication that sometimes still flashed between us. "I didn't come to ask you back. I didn't really plan to come at all. It was Fate."

"Fate?" I pushed the half-eaten sandwich away. The smell was nauseating.

He nodded slowly. "I was playing in Vegas and Barry Freiburg came through. Remember him?"

"Yes." He handled a fairly large group of second-string concert artists and seemed nice enough as I remembered. Since he was far below Jared's league we had known him only slightly.

"He mentioned the conference here and the fact that you were to be one of the speakers. Seems his wife wanted to come. She wants to write romances."

"Doesn't everyone? So you came here?"

"No, not directly. I did want to see you again...to settle things...but I...Anyway, Mac called not long after that."

"Mac is still your agent?" I asked with some shock. How could he, arguably the best classical agent in the country, continue to book Jared Granville into mindless marshmallow gigs? Unless...maybe Mac hadn't given up on Jared as much as Jared had on himself.

"Yeah. Still thinks he can bring me back to the concert stage. Anyway, he had me up for an appearance with the Cleveland Symphony. I even auditioned for them. I asked Mac to put my name in the pot for this place, too...sort of putting everything in the hands of Fate."

"So Mountain Lake Spa wanted you...and the Cleveland Symphony didn't," I said slowly, knowing what blows his pride must have taken. For a performer of his caliber to be asked to audition is insulting; to be turned down after that audition would be humiliating.

"Right."

His flat, defeated tone sliced to the very core of me. He had been brutally and cruelly broken. If I did nothing else this night I had to help him.

And I had to know two things, no matter how much the asking hurt.

He had been wise to bring me up here, but I couldn't sit still any longer. I began to pace up and down the carpeted floor. My feet had gotten very cold.

"So you just sit and wallow in self-pity."

"That's the second time you've mentioned that."

"Well, it's about time someone did. For Heaven's sake, Jared, you're one of the most gifted musicians in the country. Maybe in the world, I don't know. And here you sit, playing music you hate to a bunch of people for whom you have only contempt, simply because you lack a little backbone!"

"Elizabeth..."

"So the Cleveland Symphony turned you down; so what? You never gave a damn about what anybody in Cleveland thought. I have thought you many things, Jared, but never a coward."

He was standing now, angry, and I thought before long I would have at least one of my questions answered.

"I've lost it, Elizabeth. I can't play...My best isn't good enough for real music anymore."

"Can't?" I shrieked from the other end of the room. It was the furthest edge of the hotel and despite the thick glass wall I had the strange sensation of being on the edge of a cliff. "Or won't? You had the best technique of any pianist on the circuit. So you lost your emotions, your pretty, plastic-wrapped feelings...Well, I'm sorry, but so what? Beethoven was deaf, but he kept composing. How many times did you tell me and tell me and tell me that technique was the key? Technique!"

"I tried..." The words were weak, but his voice still had that dangerous edge. At least I was reaching him.

"Sure...for a while. It's easier to play the pitiful wreck with blasted hopes and slide through life on marshmallow music than it is to fight, isn't it?"

"I cannot see," he said in tones as icy as the moonlight outside, "why no one has murdered you yet."

"Jared...did you hit me on the head?"

The silence hung thickly between us and in those long few seconds I thought I just might die.

"No. No, Elizabeth, I did not. And you never really thought I did."

He was right. I never had, not really.

"Music was your life, Jared. You can't just throw it all away."

"Elizabeth, I've lost..."

"You've lost nothing but your nerve!"

The words hung heavy in the air, and then suddenly, eerily, the moon went behind a cloud, plunging the glass room into darkness. For a moment I shivered in primal terror, feeling in my bones waves of fear; fear of the dark, fear of my memories, fear of my emotions, the entire fear of everyone huddled in the hotel beneath me. Death and love and memories merged into one great pulsing fear, and I could feel a scream building in my throat. It was bad enough when the artificial light failed, when I was safe inside solid walls, but this sudden, preternatural darkness over all the world touched a primitive part of me...

A moment later, when the moon escaped the confining cloud and beamed down again, I felt sublimely foolish. Good grief, was I going crazy on top of everything else? I didn't react that way when the generator acted up. But I hadn't been alone with Jared when it had...

"Is that what you think?" Jared's voice was dark and constrained.

"No. That's what you think. You can play as well as you ever did, or at least you could if you practiced."

"Do you really believe that?" Sarcastically.

"Yes, I do, and Mac must too or he wouldn't keep you on his roster. He never represented anything but the best. Stop this horsing around with piano bars, Jared. Go back to what you do best."

"And if I fail?"

"Failing isn't as bad as not trying."

Incredibly, he smiled. "My God, Lillybet, that sounds like something off a calendar."

It was. I had seen it on the "Ideals" calendar in Kevin's office, and, idiot that I was, said so before thinking.

"Kevin?"

"A man in New Orleans. He wants to marry me."

"Are you going to?"

I shrugged and looked out over the frozen vista. Beyond the depression of the lake the mountains rose in staggered peaks, giving a false impression of protection. Beyond those serrated ranks were miles and miles more of mountains, then the deserted vastness of the Northwest Territories and eventually the desolation of the Arctic.

Nothing but snow and rocks, and for some strange reason I found it not only lonely but heartbreaking.

"No. I'm not."

Now. It had to be now.

"Jared...why did you leave me for Jennifer?"

The question took him off balance. He had moved over to the grand piano, his hands touching it tentatively with the shy restraint of an old lover.

"Don't you know?"

"Don't I know? Know what? I just looked up one day, and you were throwing your shirts in a suitcase, telling me you wouldn't be back." Humiliating memory scalded me. "I never knew anything was wrong between us. You were there one day, and the next day you weren't, and I never knew why. You don't have to rationalize it, Jared. Just tell me why."

"You mean it..." he murmured in wonder. "You really don't know."

"You thought I did?"

"I don't see how you couldn't. You said one day I just wasn't there. Well, you hadn't been there for me in months."

My knees failed me. I sank into a chair, wishing myself a thousand miles away. "What? I never went anywhere."

"No, you didn't leave the apartment, but you went in to your typewriter every day. Between you and your book there was nothing left for me. Jennifer...I thought Jennifer needed me."

Needed him...

Needed him?

All the times I reached out, and he wasn't there, the way I had felt only half alive after he left, how I had looked so hungrily at men who resembled him, just pretending for a minute...

"And you thought I didn't?" I said in a tiny voice. "You were...*piqued* because I paid attention to my art? What about all the hours and days and months I just sat and watched you practice? It goes both ways, Jared; when you had your music you didn't need anything else."

He looked startled. The blue moonlight had bleached his face of any color, and I remembered Anita's tall, pale man.

"That's what Jennifer said. Later."

"I'm sorry she died. I'm sorry she wasn't right for you."

"Maybe I wasn't right for her."

I stood on very shaky legs. I had asked my two questions. I didn't want to know any more. "I'm going downstairs."

"Elizabeth..."

"Please, Jared. I don't want to talk any more."

"All right, but I am going to take you to your room. Remember, there is a murderer running around loose."

Incredibly, I had forgotten. Past misery had completely blotted out present reality.

"There's no need."

"Maybe, but I'm still going to do it." He grabbed my elbow, but this time it was gently; there were no signals. "I guess you'll be going tomorrow."

"As soon as the road is clear. Unless Hunter arrests me."

"There's no way he can do that. You're innocent."

"I wish he believed that."

"Pete's full of hot air. And you were right; he is bucking for a promotion. You'll be all right, Lillybet, I promise you." He said in a gentle tone that almost broke my heart. Hesitantly, he placed a whisper of a kiss right at my hairline. "I probably won't see you again. Tomorrow, Finlay will need all the help he can get."

There was nothing more to say yet I couldn't let go, not just yet.

"Jared...I'm glad we met again. I really do wish you the best." Such pitiful words, I knew even as they left my mouth they weren't what I really wanted to say.

"And I you, Lillybet," he said with a quicksilver smile that wrenched at my heart. "I'll be looking for your next book."

"And I want to hear about your next concert."

The silence descended again, trapping us in an embarrassing moment of silence. What was the correct etiquette for this situation? A handshake? A kiss?

Nothing?

I found myself waiting for a kiss, and since it was a night of magic, my wish came true. Jared gently placed his hands on my shoulders and lowered his lips to mine. It was a kiss of tenderness, not of passion, and too soon over. When he straightened his face was rigid and harsh, his eyes hooded.

"Come on. It'll be faster if we go down in the service elevator."

I took one last look at the cold, enchanted fairyland outside while Jared locked the big double doors. Not all fairy tales had happy endings, I remembered.

Escorting without touching, Jared led us through the enormous, clinical kitchen to the elevator. The silence was so intense I could hear the doors shutting far beneath us then the faint whine of the elevator as the car rose toward us and at last, the faint whoosh of the doors opening.

Taylor Huggins leaned against the back of the car, her mouth open. The front of her red turtleneck was wet enough to glisten in the faint light.

Only as she began to slide inexorably toward the floor did I realize that she was dead.

Chapter Ten

"She must have died almost instantly," Sergeant Hunter said, scowling directly at me. Having another murder, one for which I could not possibly be responsible, had not improved his mood.

"So when we heard the doors close beneath us, she must have just been stabbed," Jared murmured.

"Please, Mr. Granville…" Anita shivered and patted my hand in one complicated motion. "We mustn't upset Elizabeth any more."

I took another sip of brandy. It felt like fire going down. I had screamed until Jared had been forced to slap me. After that, I was a little hazy about the exact order of things. There had seemed to be a lot of people around — the Mounties, muscular bellboys who had been pressed into duty as hotel security, Dr. Wilcox tut-tutting little whisky-scented clouds as he pronounced Taylor Huggins officially dead…

Now, after what seemed to be days up in that horrible, sterile kitchen, we were in the comparatively sybaritic warmth of the Cariboo Suite. Someone had brought me a brandy, head injury or no, then when that one was gone, had brought me another. I had stopped crying almost immediately, but still Jared had insisted that Anita be called. Of course Bernie had come, too.

"Well, this knocks your theory of someone trying to kill our 'Fabulous Four' into a cocked hat," Bernie said with an almost ghoulish relief. "That young woman never wrote a word for Wingate Romances."

Sergeant Hunter was not amused. Sitting behind the delicate desk he scowled at all of us impartially. "Maybe so, but she was sure going to write about you all. There must be a lot of stuff in her notebook about Wingate and 'The Fabulous Four'."

He made it sound like an insult.

"Her notebook?" Anita asked.

He nodded. "Surely you saw her carrying it around. A battered looking green steno pad. Every time she talked to someone she scribbled in it. Everyone's mentioned it."

"Do you have the notebook?" Bernie asked. "I'd like to know..."

"No, Mr. Wingate, I do not, and even if I did, I couldn't let you see it. It would be evidence."

"I have a right to know what people are saying about me and my company..."

"Do you know who has the notebook, Sergeant?"

"Of course I do, Mrs. Wingate. The murderer."

His face dark with thought, Jared had been pacing, as if he were the one who disliked being confined. Suddenly, he settled gracefully on the arm of my chair and began to rub my back in lazy circles.

"Taylor Huggins was really getting in the way of your investigation, wasn't she, Pete?"

"Damn right. Couldn't take a step without her poking and prying and sticking her nose in...Bloody nuisance, she was."

"And you're glad she's out of the way?"

Hunter's eyes narrowed suspiciously. "What are you

getting at?"

"Just demonstrating how easy it is to appear to have a motive for murder when you are obviously as innocent as could be."

I stared up at Jared in awe. He was fighting for me, trying to convince Hunter that I wasn't guilty. Who was this strange new Jared Granville? Had he gone through the fires of failure and loss and really emerged a new, finer human being? Did I dare trust enough to risk finding out?

Or was he concealing something?

I couldn't help but remember how confident he had sounded when he promised me that I wouldn't be arrested for Jane's and Clement's murders. How could he have been so sure?

There was one sure way. He could commit another murder, one totally unrelated, while I had an unimpeachable alibi—him.

I shook my head. The brandy must be affecting me. He couldn't have killed Taylor Huggins. We had been together when she had been stabbed.

When we thought she had been stabbed.

What if she had one of those weird blood diseases where the blood doesn't clot? There would be no way to tell that without all kinds of exotic tests; besides, how could Jared have known about it?

Unless, she told him.

Ridiculous. That kind of thing happened only in mystery novels. This was real, uncomfortably, really *real*.

But Jared had promised.

He could have had an accomplice. He had always

been able to charm just about anyone into doing just about anything. He had been gone while I sat in plain view in the bar, but for how long? I had never had any time sense, but in spite of how long it had seemed, not that much time could have passed — ten minutes, fifteen? Was that was long enough to...to do what? Make arrangements to meet Taylor Huggins, only to have someone else show up?

While we were together — and could alibi each other — his accomplice could have...

I shook my head. I had passed beyond speculation into insanity. Jared committing murder just to clear my name? Ridiculous.

And even if on the wildest off chance it were true, I would deny it to my dying breath, I decided, making a commitment I didn't even know was in question.

"Lillybet, you're as pale as a ghost. What's the matter?"

I couldn't verbalize what I had been thinking, so instead I said the first thing that popped into my mind. That has always been a bad habit of mine. "Is Vanessa all right? Has someone checked on her?"

Sergeant Hunter's eyes flickered. "Miss Mangold is fine, Miss MacAllister. It's kind of you to be so concerned."

He thought I was asking because I wanted to murder her. I knew it as well as I knew my own name. I could feel the blood rushing to my face. "I...I didn't mean...I...You've got it wrong."

"You're so tired you don't know what you're saying, Lillybet. She's got to get some rest, Pete. Can't we let the ladies go to their rooms?"

"No. There's a lot we need to know yet..."

"Officer Hunter," Anita said in her most patrician voice, "I assure you that we are not going anywhere. It is late, and Elizabeth is ill. We will see you in the morning."

Not even the RCMP could stand up to Anita Wingate when her mind was made up. Hunter suddenly reversed his decision.

I should have felt suspicious then.

"You're right, Jerry. There's no need to keep the ladies up." He called to one of the husky bellboys/security men to escort us to our rooms.

"I'll take them..."

"No, stay here. I need to talk to you. They'll be all right. Come look at this."

Jared obediently walked over to the desk while Anita and our husky escort hauled me to my feet. It was unexpectedly necessary. The brandies had settled in the area of my knees. My first few steps were wobbly, but by the time we reached the door, I was feeling as strong as could be expected.

"Good night..." I said hesitantly.

Jared never even turned around.

* * *

Feeling strangely empty, I leaned back against the door and automatically snapped the chain home. It had taken some doing to convince Anita to go with the security man instead of staying with me, but I knew I would go completely mad if she stayed and dithered on and on about the lack of morals and standards in the modern world—as if multiple murder were nothing more than a matter of manners.

As for Jared...

Somehow I thought I should feel happier, lighter, freer, but I didn't. An old question had been answered and all strings left dangling from the past had been wrapped into a nice, neat knot.

Why, then, did I want to cry?

Drat it, I would not cry! At least, not here, not now. Things would look better once I got home. This had been a horrible experience, and in my own little apartment with my own little flower-filled patio I would be able to see more clearly. It would be safe, even if it were a little lonely.

There was always Kevin.

Maybe I had been unfair to Kevin. Maybe...

No. Not that. No substitutions.

Murders, snow, Jared...It was more than one woman should be expected to bear. I turned out the light and walked to the window. From this point of view the moonlight was less spectacular. Leprous patches of yellow disfigured the snow. Only the far mountains, remote and unapproachable, remained that beautiful, pristine blue.

My mind ran on tracks I didn't like. I didn't want to think about Jared and the unchangeable past. Actually, I wanted to sleep, but knew I was too keyed up for that. There are few worse fates than to lie tossing and wakeful when there is something you don't want to think about, for usually then you can think of nothing else.

If I really intended—if I were permitted—to be off first thing in the morning, as soon as the snowplows came through, I needed to be packed. I wandered around aimlessly, picking things up and putting them down again and not really accomplishing anything. Finally, I stopped and sat down in the easy chair. Mindless action wasn't the answer.

How much I had dreaded coming to this silly conference and for all the wrong reasons. In retrospect, all my objections seemed so shallow and petty. I didn't like the cold. So, it was April, and under normal circumstances there would have been heat. I hadn't wanted to talk about my writers' block. Who did?

I hadn't liked Jane or Clement or Vanessa...But neither had I ever wanted to see any of them dead.

Someone had, though.

I gnawed on a fingernail and thought. Neither Jane nor Clement had been especially popular, but who had disliked them enough to kill them?

And how did Taylor Huggins fit into this? If anything, she had seemed to be more against Wingate Romances than for it. Enough against it to want Jane and Clement dead, maybe Vanessa too?

If appearances were to be believed, Vanessa would have been the next victim if she had opened her door. Instead, I had blundered into the middle of it and gotten knocked on the head.

If that were the murderer, why wasn't I dead?

If that weren't the murderer, why had they disappeared, leaving me lying on the floor?

Why?

Try another tack. Was there anything that connected Jane and Clement and Vanessa? They didn't seem to share anything in common except that they were all romance writers and part of the so-called "Fabulous Four" of Wingate Romances.

So was I.

Jane and Clement had been murdered, Vanessa had been in a questionable situation, and I had escaped with only a knot on my head.

Why?

How were we different? There had been rumors that Jane was going to leave Wingate, but Clement had never said anything about changing publishers, and I was just glad that Bernie still wanted me. Besides, that was a ridiculous train of thought. Not only was Bernie totally incapable of murder, he'd be killing the very company he was working so desperately to save.

It was late. I should pack. I should undress. I should go to bed. There were lots of things I should do, but somehow I just couldn't let go. There was something, some small little fact that was lurking just beyond the edge of conscious thought and once it was caught, everything would be answered.

Right.

I moved on to another fingernail. Outside the moon arced on across the sky. One by one the hotel lights went out, and once again the world was blue.

Why wasn't I dead?

Hadn't I sold enough? I knew that my books, one a romance and one not, didn't stand up much against their hundreds of releases, but through the accident of a single best-seller list, I had been absorbed to become part of "The Fabulous Four". Bernie still had great hopes for me.

If the motive for Jane and Clement's murders were jealousy of them and their sales, I would indeed be a prime suspect, but why on earth would I want to kill Taylor Huggins? In any case, I knew I hadn't done it, even if no one else believed me. No one except Jared...

Had it really been the murderer knocking at Vanessa's door? I sort of felt it had to be; who else would knock me over the head for coming out just then?

But if that were the case, *why wasn't I dead?*

My head started to throb. Somehow in the strange, magical, out-of-time interlude with Jared on the seventh floor I had forgotten it hurt, and in the horrible aftermath, there had been other things to occupy the attention. I tried to ignore it.

Why had Taylor Huggins been killed? She was an annoyance and a pest and a rotten reporter, but were those really motives for murder?

Or had she just been in the wrong place at the wrong time?

For that matter, what had she been doing in the service elevator?

Ignoring my headache wasn't working. I got up and took another aspirin. Then, as I was turning off the bathroom light, another, infinitely more ghastly light went on in my head. I stopped short in the middle of the room, brought to a dead halt by the solid wall of an unbelievable idea.

Bending slowly, as if my entire body were rusted stiff, I picked up the manuscript of *A Man of Honor* that Bernie had so cavalierly tossed into the wastebasket. As if I had never touched the like before, I slowly riffled through the pages. They were slick and crisp beneath my fingers, and they crackled like fire as my hands closed convulsively.

I had never looked at it like that, had never really seen the one thing that made me different from the others.

I had never thought...

Chapter Eleven

I don't know how long I stood there with those pages crumpled in my fists, but finally the realization came that the unspeakable thing I was thinking could be—had to be—the truth, at least the beginning of the truth.

I had to tell someone. There had to be someone with whom I could talk this through, someone who would tell me I was wrong.

My fingers were numb, but I managed to reach the sleepy-sounding operator.

"Jared...Jerry Grant, please."

The line shrilled as a phone somewhere rang and rang without answer. Irrationally, I felt deserted. Where was he when I needed him?

Could he still be with Sergeant Hunter? I got the operator back and asked for the Cariboo Suite. There was no answer there, either, and that made me angry. They were public servants. How dare they be missing when I needed to talk to them?

I didn't want to be the only one to carry this dreadful suspicion.

Finally, I realized that the manuscript was still crushed in my other hand. I had to force the fingers to relax and free the crumpled sheets. They fell around my feet like monstrous snowflakes.

Five minutes. I'd wait five minutes, then...

Then what?

Never had five minutes passed so slowly. I dithered in little chores, picking up the scattered papers and packing away the typewriter, folding clothes and emptying drawers. Thinking that my silver sequins were a bit gaudy for the occasion, I reached for slacks and sweater. No use even thinking of going to bed until I had talked this over with someone.

And then there was a hesitant knock at my door.

I swallowed heavily. There was no way I could pretend I was asleep. The room light would show clearly through the frosted glass transom. I put down my jeans and tried to answer in a normal voice.

"Who is it?"

"Elizabeth? It is I—Anita. I saw your light was on and just wanted to check on you..."

I swallowed again even though my mouth was almost powdery dry. Not now, for Heaven's sake. "I'm fine, Anita. Just finishing up a little packing. Thank you."

"Are you all right, dear? I'd like to be sure..."

"It's late, Anita."

"I won't stay but a minute..."

"Just one moment, Elizabeth," she all but pleaded. "I promised that policeman I would check on you. Please don't make me go get a bellman to open the door..."

She was more than capable of bringing half the staff up here if I refused to open up, either that or a battering ram. I should have known she wouldn't go away until she achieved what she wanted, so I shrugged and opened the door. Anita didn't want to harm me.

She stepped in and closed the door behind her. She hadn't changed. Her long silk shirtwaist was the color of blood. Funny, I didn't remember it being that red.

"I just thought I'd look in and see how you were doing before I turned in. You're still dressed...You need to get some rest, my dear. It's been a very stressful night."

"I was just doing some packing..."

I had always thought it wasn't difficult to read Anita's thought processes. She could dispense the polite chatter with the best of them, but if she wanted something it was one or two polite sentences, then *boom*, right to the heart of it.

She perched on the edge of the dresser and looked me squarely in the eye. "How did you enjoy your dinner with that piano player?"

"It was all right. He used to be one of the finest concert pianists in the world, Anita."

"And now he is playing in the cocktail bar?" One delicate eyebrow arched with ruthless eloquence. "Well, I know it is sometimes painful to turn loose of the past, Elizabeth, but if it must be done, it must be done."

There was nothing to be gained by waiting. Suddenly, the tensions of the night were too much to bear, and I felt I couldn't wait any longer to know if my wild idea were right or wrong. "Anita, where's Bernie? I need to talk to him."

"I wouldn't advise it, my dear. Bernard was in the shower when I left. I just ran over quickly to make sure you were all right." Her eyes flicked appraisingly over me. "I meant to tell you earlier, that truly is a stunning dress. What a shame you didn't get to wear it to something truly elegant. Want a zip or are you meeting your piano player again?"

Her words were like ice chips—cold and hard, and they cut more deeply than I had expected.

"No. I shan't be seeing Jared again."

"Then let me unzip you..."

I stepped backwards. Getting out of this dress alone would be more of an athletic contest than getting into it had been, but now the flimsy material was somehow like armor. "No, not now...Can we just talk for a minute?"

"Of course, dear, if you really want to. I was hoping that we could have some time together during this ghastly conference. It seems there's never any time for us to chat." She moved toward the easy chair, and her gaze fell on the empty wastebasket. "I am glad to see you remembered to rescue that manuscript. Bernard really shouldn't have behaved like that. He's an excellent businessman, but sometimes he's just so irrational...I really do not know what I'm going to do with him." Her voice held a slight quiver of emotion.

Her emotion resonated in me too, because now I knew my wild, unbelievable theories weren't true. Worse, I now knew the truth.

I took another step backwards. "Anita, do you think..."

"What, Elizabeth?"

I didn't say what I had been so carefully rehearsing. To my horror my mouth acted independently and said the words that had been burning in my mind.

"Why did you kill them?"

* * *

Anita's composed expression did not alter, and for

one soaring moment I hoped I had been wrong.

"So you did figure everything out," she said at last. Her voice was thick with regret. "I was afraid you might when you started asking questions about that door. You always were such a clever girl."

"Why?" I asked with real grief. "It wasn't just the romances, was it?"

She looked at me as if I had disappointed her. "Of course it was. I tried my best to talk Bernard out of this dreadful idea of publishing nothing but romances, but he wouldn't listen to me."

"But is that a reason to kill?"

Anita ignored me, words long bottled up pouring out of her. "Perhaps Wingate Publications didn't make as much money as some of the other independent houses, but it had a reputation for quality. We were someone!"

I stared at her. My stomach knotted painfully.

"But Bernard always wanted to make more money, as if money were the only thing that mattered. I could never convince him that status and behavior mattered more than money. He said it was all for me, so I could have the best." Her voice was tragic.

"He loves you, Anita."

"No, he doesn't!" she snapped imperiously. "How could he prostitute Wingate Publications, destroy everything that was good and uplifting and decent about the company if he loved me?"

"Bernie loves business... Romances are big business now..."

She ignored me. "I could have married a drug dealer or a gambler from my old neighborhood and had ten times more money than Bernard could ever give me. Do you know what status is, Elizabeth? Real status?"

"No."

"Having people look up to you. Being just a little bit better than the common herd. Being a someone, a someone who makes life better, who contributes to the finer things." She turned her back to me and stared out the window. "Jane and Clement and Vanessa never contributed anything but a bunch of trash about people who flaunt their emotions and think only with their genitals."

"Is Vanessa all right?"

"Of course. The silly bitch has herself so locked up and guarded that not even God could get to her now."

Thank goodness for that.

"And Taylor Huggins?"

"That cheap tramp? She tried to seduce Bernard...not that he would pay any attention to her, of course. He knew from the beginning that all she wanted was to write for Wingate Romances." She spit out the name as if it were bitter.

"So you killed her. And Jane. And Clement."

"I had no choice."

"And that's why you didn't kill me."

"My dear, I never had any intention of harming you. After *A Woman of Quality* I could see that you were going to be a great writer, perhaps one of the literary giants of the century. I realize that Bernard forced you into writing that dreadful romance, and of course I don't hold it against you, but the wonderful thing was that you never stopped work on *A Man of Honor*. That showed your true quality, unlike those pushy cows downstairs or that obnoxious reporter."

"All for a book..." I murmured. I felt sick to my stomach.

"That reporter even brought her manuscript with her," Anita said with a *moue* of distaste. "A great thick thing called *Passions in the Afternoon..*"

"Her manuscript? She wrote a romance novel?"

"Yes, printed on pale pink paper, if you can imagine. These people have no taste at all. She even bragged about how many love scenes there were in it." Anita shuddered. "It was fit for nothing but burning."

"You burned it?"

"No, but it will be. I wrapped it and her notebook in an old newspaper and dumped it down the trash chute. Just where rubbish like that belongs." For a moment she looked proud and quite self-righteous, and then her face fell, leaving her expression almost grief-stricken. "I'm just so sorry that you figured everything out..."

Something in her voice subtly altered, and I shivered. I couldn't look at her, but I had to keep her talking.

"It was you who knocked at Vanessa's door and hit me on the head."

She nodded. "With my shoe." Lifting her skirt she displayed a rather *avant-garde* wedge decorated with brilliants. When she had brought them back from Paris I had thought them terribly cute. "I hated to hurt you, but I was really trying to protect you. If that silly woman had just answered her door, and you had waited..."

"Then you hid in the laundry room after you hit

me."

"Yes. My room was already locked and I heard the elevator opening."

"And Taylor Huggins?"

Anita shrugged her shoulders with an elegant gesture. "Greedy little bitch. All I had to do was whisper that I would make sure Bernie would publish her, and she would meet me anywhere."

"You murdered her just because she wanted to write romances?"

"Of course not." She looked shocked. "Only a madman would do that; think of the slaughter it would entail. There is a place for people who like that kind of trash...just not at Wingate Publications."

I opened my mouth to say something, then thought better of it and simply asked, "Then why?"

"To give you an alibi, of course. The police really did suspect you, which is something I would never have anticipated, but then they can't be too intelligent if they're policemen, can they?" Anita smiled dazzlingly. "It was no trouble to find out that you were with your piano player, so I decided to kill two birds with one stone. If you were with someone they trusted, you couldn't be the murderer."

I stared at her in horror. "What about the tall, pale man?"

"Who?"

"You said you saw a tall, pale man."

She shrugged dismissively. "Oh, that was nothing, just an invention of the moment, to draw any possible suspicion away from me. I honestly never dreamed that

Clement or the piano player would be suspected, but it didn't work out too badly, did it?"

There was a smile in her voice, and I thought of how I had agonized over those careless words. *Forgive me, Jared...*

"What do we do now, Anita? You know this can't go on."

"I made a mistake, Elizabeth. I underestimated you. I never dreamed you would..." She gave herself a sorrowful little shake and went on. "It will be a great loss to the literary world that *A Man of Honor* was never finished, but I can't leave any loose ends. You understand that, don't you? You can see that it's up to me to save Wingate Publications and all that it stands for. Think of all those other good authors who write quality literature whom it will publish. I'm sorry, Elizabeth...I'm so sorry. You just shouldn't have meddled..." She sounded truly distressed, but still she pulled a knife from up her long sleeve.

A wooden handled steak knife.

This was it. My time had just run out.

"A plebeian instrument, but a very efficient one. I borrowed a handful from the service dresser."

"Anita..." I think I said. My voice was more of a squeak. I cleared my throat and began over again. How long would it take Bernie to finish his shower and come looking for his wife?

I started to back up very slowly, my eyes never leaving the raised blade. I wouldn't have any chance in hand-to-hand combat with her, so my best bet was to run. The door was closed, but the chain was off. If I could just move quickly enough...

"Please do not underestimate me, Elizabeth. I started thinking about what must be done when Bernard first mentioned changing to romances exclusively. It is not a whim; I tried every other possible way first. I do not enjoy killing, Elizabeth; believe me, I never thought it would go this far, but I cannot stop now. Can't you see that? Someone has to maintain the standards of Wingate Publications..."

She started toward me. After a terrifying second of paralysis I realized it was too late to run. I had waited too long, and the door was an impossible distance away. I could never make it...

For the third time that evening the hotel was plunged into sudden darkness. This time it stayed. Anita must have been as startled as I, for in the moonlight that spilled in through the uncurtained window I could see her standing immobile. The blue light glinted wickedly off the blade in her hand.

It was as much of a miracle as I dared hope for. I dashed into the dark. Strange how proportions seem to change when there is no light. I crashed into a great many more things than I remembered being there in the light, but at last I had the door open and was out.

The hallway wasn't as dark as I had feared it might be. The small frosted window near the elevator bank allowed a faint glow of moonlight to seep in. There was enough to light my path, but also enough to betray my presence.

Anita was thudding along behind me. She even swore after one particularly loud bump, using words I had never heard, but then she didn't have to be quiet to survive. Like I did.

Of course the elevators would be useless. Somewhere a girl was screaming...one of the elevator operators caught between floors. I couldn't spare her much pity.

There was a set of stairs leading down just past the elevators. I groped down them, clinging to the rail. Unfortunately, there was no corresponding flight going up, which was odd, but this was an old hotel. If this stair only reached the lobby, maybe I could find a service stair that would take me back up to the third floor and the Mounties.

The steps ended, and the glare of moonlight through the tall arched windows made it all too clear where I was. To the right were the closed and locked glass doors of the Empress dining room; to the left was the grand staircase that led down to the lobby.

The entire first floor was flooded with cold blue light that made my sequined dress glow as if electrified.

* * *

I hung there, gripping the rail for grim death, undecided as to whether I should go back up into that thick darkness and risk Anita wouldn't find the downward stair, or to gamble that I could get down that dreadfully bright grand stair and get lost in the lobby.

Too close behind to be comfortable, there was the definite scrape of a shoe on the bristly carpet.

So Anita had remembered that sometimes the hunter has to be as quiet as the hunted.

I skittered forward on tiptoe, trying to run as quietly

as possible past the grand staircase, through the writing room beyond and around the corner into the deepest shadow I could find.

At first I could hear nothing but the thunderous pumping of my heart. Could Anita hear it? It almost sounded loud enough to wake the entire hotel.

"Elizabeth?" It was just the ghost of a whisper, hardly more than a sigh.

I ventured a quick peep around the shielding corner. Anita's red silk didn't stand out as well in the moonlight as my silver sequins, but there was enough light for me to see her standing at the head of the grand staircase. The knife in her hand glowed as if it had been forged of pure light. If only she would go down that way and let me escape in the other direction.

Anita took two steps down the carpeted stairs, and that was all I needed. About fifteen yards ahead of me was a set of utilitarian-looking swinging doors, maybe the service stairs? I could get to the Mounties...

The doors shrieked like a starving hawk. They could probably hear it all the way over to Hillside House.

I couldn't go anywhere but forward, and it didn't lead anywhere near the Mounties. There were stairs all right, but the faint flash of light through the doors showed that they went only down.

Hanging onto the rail with clammy fingers, I stumbled forward into the absolute blackness as much on all fours as upright. There was no choice. I couldn't go back out into that all-revealing moonlight, but could I go into that enveloping darkness? It wrapped around me and clung like a bad dream, squeezing out the air drowning me...Even though I could touch nothing but the rail and the steps beneath me, I felt as if I were being buried alive, which is anyone's—claustrophobe or not—nightmare.

I tried to tell myself that the fear I felt was only in my mind; this was nothing but an enclosed service stair. On the other hand, behind me was a very real and present danger. I had to go forward.

These steps were different, they were cold and slick and metal edges. There were two short flights, with a 180º turn in the middle. Somehow I ended up making most of the trip sitting down, creeping forward as quietly as possible. It was not a way of travel I would recommend. I could feel the metal rims catching on my silver sequins and pulling them off; so much for my fabulous famous-author gown.

I'd be lucky if it didn't turn into a shroud.

The stairs ended abruptly in another set of swinging doors. I ran into them before I knew they were there, but luckily this time there was no screech. They shivered silently as if freshly oiled. The darkness was absolute.

The acrid smell of chlorine filled the air. The swimming pool! I had completely forgotten. The first day here—good grief, just *yesterday*? - I had only glanced at it. Now I tried desperately to remember how it looked.

Built in the last few years, the pool addition was an enormous room glassed in on three sides. There was a huge pool with a tile walkway going all around it. I couldn't remember anything else.

If necessary, I supposed I could hide in the water.

Did Anita know how to swim?

Above me there was a predatory screech, and th
stairwell glowed faintly with a spill of weak moonligh
Anita must be right on my tail. Curse the woman, woul
she never give up? There was no way she could get awa
with this murder.

Wasn't there? Hadn't she gotten away with all th
others? No one had ever suspected her but me.

But she couldn't kill me...Heroines never died, and
was a heroine, wasn't I? I mean, this was my life, right?

And a fine mess I had made of it, too.

Jared...

Jared would find me.

Some heroine I was. Jared never wanted to see m
again. Oh, when he found out I'd been killed, he'
probably grieve a little for me, but...

He'd never know how much I still loved him.

Honestly, until that clarifying moment, I hadn
either.

Well, the only thing I could do was to surviv
Nothing could be straightened out unless I lived.

I slipped through the doors. They whooshed softl
back and forth as if breathing.

The pool area was a fairyland. The moon shon
brightly through the glass walls, illuminating the entir
room with a hard and pitiless light. By now the rags c
storm clouds were gone, and the sky was a canopy c
sequin-studded navy silk.

Apparently the power had been cut off completely i
here, for the air was frigid. Teeth chattering convulsivel
I shivered in my off-the-shoulder creation and longed fc
my jacket, a blanket, any kind of warmth.

No, that wasn't true. I was longing for Jared's arms around me.

And to get that, I had to survive.

The water was more reluctant than the air to give up its warmth to the leaching cold. Great swirls of shimmering fog rose from the surface, combining with the moonlight to create a beautiful but incredibly eerie landscape. It was almost like a medieval artist's vision of Heaven—or Hell, otherworldly, insubstantial and frightening.

Still, it was my only hope. There had to be another way out of here, if I could just stay alive long enough to find it. There wasn't much of a walk along the edges—no more than a yard and a half or so, and all of it tiled. I'd have to be very careful or end up in the drink.

Taking a deep breath, I slipped into the fog, trying not to fall into the pool and to avoid the brightest areas. It was nightmarish. There were not enough vapors to hide me, only enough to hide what I needed to see. At least here the silver dress was less of a drawback, for the entire roiling mass of fog glinted silver.

Beneath my feet the glazed tile was slick with a thin film of moisture. It was like walking on wet glass. Taking a few precious seconds, I crouched in a shadow and slipped out of my shoes. The wet floor was cursedly cold on my stocking feet, but at least I wouldn't clatter against the soaking tiles and maybe it could give me a little better balance.

Right now I needed all the advantages I could get.

"Elizabeth?" Anita's voice slithered through the fog. I don't know if it was the product of the over-emotional moment or a property of the cavernous glass room, but I had never heard such a horrible sound in my life.

Huddling in the shadows I started to repeat a prayer I hadn't thought of in years.

"I'm so sorry, Elizabeth. I didn't want to frighten you. Why did you have to figure it all out? You must see it's so much better my way...I'm so sorry you have to die but I promise you it won't hurt. My uncle learned the trick in prison. One quick thrust and your heart stops and you won't even know it happened..." She whispered soothingly, cajolingly, the words pouring out like fresh cream.

I didn't dare move, didn't dare breathe, and didn't dare think. I had never been so close to death before, and oddly enough, that gave new focus to my life. They say that when you are drowning your entire life flashes in front of your face. The fog wasn't thick enough to hide in let alone drown in, but the only thing I could think of was Jared.

Now, I could admit even to myself that I hadn't wanted him to leave, not two and a half years ago, not tonight, but both times I had been too proud to ask him to stay. Would he have? Would I ever have the opportunity to ask him again? Even more tragic, if I died tonight, would he ever guess how I felt?

"Elizabeth?"

For a moment the shifting curtains of vapor treacherously parted, allowing the moonlight to illuminate us in brilliant blue. Anita was so close I could have touched her.

She smiled. It was terrible.

I moved quickly, but she was faster than I. The knife flashed like molten metal in the moonlight, and there was a strip of fire searing into my arm. Almost immediately I could feel my blood reveling in its freedom, bubbling to the surface and sliding in a hot sticky flood down my arm.

Biting back a cry of pain I stumbled and slipped along the wall, heading for the far end of the room where the fog seemed to be thicker, like a wounded animal will head for cover. My arm was on fire, yet conversely drowning in its own blood, immobile but twitching with pain.

I stopped. There was a shadow here where the fog was thicker. Mouth held grimly shut lest I cry out with the dizzying, nauseating pain, I stood as still as possible, trying to sort out the eddying whispers of sound that floated through the room.

Jared...

Jared. How many times does false pride keep us from what we really want? And how many times do we learn it too late? His name, repeated over and over, had replaced that half-forgotten prayer as my litany of protection.

"I didn't mean to hurt you, Elizabeth," Anita said, and there was genuine regret in her voice. "Come here, and I'll make the hurting stop. It's better if it's over soon..."

She was coming closer. I could feel it.

"You can appreciate that it must be done. You'd tell everything, and my work isn't finished. Literature..."

Facing death has a strange effect on people.

Suddenly, I was as angry as I had ever been. The *nerve* of her!

"Who gives you the right to decide?" I roared. "People have a right to live their lives as they want."

The acoustics of the glass room were unbelievable; the ricocheting sound made it seem as if I were in a hundred places and yet still no place in particular. If I could get her talking, delay her, maybe someone would come. If not, and it truly were my time to die, perhaps I could grab her and pull her into deep water and do my best to see that she didn't survive to kill again.

"It's my duty." Her words were clipped as if she were stating a truth so obvious even a child should see it. "Someone has to see that things are done properly, with some decorum and propriety." She sounded more aggressive now. "There's no need for anyone to be ignorant and vulgar. If I can pull myself out of the gutter, anyone can. I have to help them, don't you see?"

"Not everyone has your dream. People want different things..."

For just a moment her head broke free of the fog and floated there like a pale echo of the moon above. The face had Anita's features, but they were somehow different. However mad she was, though, her voice was heart-breakingly sane. "Really, Elizabeth. We can't have the little nobodies of the world deciding how things are to be. Vulgarians... There are standards."

"Your standards," I said, inching backwards. The pain in my arm was making me dizzy.

"I truly didn't want to hurt you." She was coming toward me, seemingly nothing more than a face floating on the fog, but somewhere in there she held a knife, a knife with which she was going to kill me. "You wrote that lovely book, and you were going to write another and another...I saw how Bernard's silly plan upset you..."

"What about Bernie? Does he know you kill people?"

"Of course not. And he won't, because as soon as he realizes that publishing all that trash is vulgar and unacceptable, I'll stop. I'm sorry, Elizabeth," she said briskly, "but he will be wondering where I am. Let me finish this so I can get back to him."

Bernie! Maybe he would suspect, call the Mounties...

It was a blasted hope. Bernie could be a darling, but he was undeniably dense in matters outside business. He never noticed anything unless it hit him over the head. There was no help coming.

"Anita..." My voice was nothing but a whimper.

"That's enough, Mrs. Wingate." A low, growling baritone cut through the floating vapors like a benediction.

"Jared..." I murmured then shrieked, "Look out, darling! She's got a knife!"

The fog swirled and swayed, and through some strange magic parted so that I could see everything. Panther-sure on the slick tiles Jared crept forward, his hand extended. I held my breath. Surely he had heard me? One quick slash with that knife and he would never be able to play the piano again.

"Jared!" I cried. "Be careful!"

"Are you all right, Lillybet?" His gaze was focused on Anita like a cat's on a bird.

"I'm hurt, darling. She cut my arm."

"You are interrupting in a private matter," Anita said at her most regal. "Surely you do not grasp what is at stake."

"It's all over, Mrs. Wingate." Jared's voice dropped another tone. "Give me the knife."

And he kept coming, the fog swirling around his legs.

Then, in a moment that will live in my nightmares for the rest of my life, Anita changed. Her beautifully composed face flattened into a bestial snarl, her wide-set eyes flashing ferally in the cold moonlight, making her look like some sort of wild beast. She gave a hair-raising growl from deep in her chest, and raising the knife high above her head, charged Jared.

I tried to scream, but had no voice. The vapors, thicker than ever, rose and swelled and choked me, holding me immobile like some enchanted vine.

The man I loved was going to be murdered by a madwoman before my staring eyes, and I could do nothing...

Chapter Twelve

Anita never got within striking distance of Jared. He was braced to deflect her attack, but she never reached him. Her pretty, brilliant-heeled evening slippers betrayed her, twisting on the wet tiles, and sending her sprawling across them with a sound I shall never forget. Her head struck the pool coping with enough force to fracture her skull. Despite the best efforts of Dr. Wilcox, she died several hours later without ever regaining consciousness.

Ignoring her, Jared stepped directly over her prone body. "Lillybet! Where are you?" he cried, but his voice sounded like it was coming from a long way away. The grasping fog was darker and holding me more and more tightly...

As a romantic heroine I am something of a bust. Instead of coming forward for an emotional clinch with Jared, I fainted, crumpling—as they later told me—directly into the pool. All I remember is that the rapidly cooling water brought my senses back with a vicious jerk. Choking and gasping, I swallowed a lot of the pool trying to surface. The pain in my arm was indescribable, but at least it made me know I was still alive.

Without a pause Jared arced gracefully into the water, and after two or three strong strokes, had his arms safely around me.

"It's all right, Lillybet. I'm here."

"Don't ever go away again, Jared. I love you," I

murmured around a mouthful of water and fainted away once more.

* * *

Is that the end of the story?

Yes and no. It was the end of the murders at Mountain Lake Spa and the death knell for Wingate Romances. Bernie never officially stopped publishing and none of his remaining stable officially quit him, but within a year or so everything simply faded to nothing, and he just drifted away. The last I heard of him he was teaching a class in romance writing in Key West.

It seems I was in more than one kind of danger that night. In spite of my unquestionable innocence in Taylor Huggins' death Sergeant Hunter was convinced that I had murdered Jane and Clement, and he was determined to prove it. Jared, equally if quixotically convinced of my innocence, had argued and argued with him. They had argued so long that it almost cost my life.

Only through chance had they seen Anita chasing me, knife in hand, and only the shrieking of the stair doors had told them of our location. From that moment on, Jared told me later, he and the Mounties had never been more than a couple of yards behind us, though the darkness hampered as well as concealed them.

"I wasn't going to let anything happen to you, Lillybet," Jared murmured laying yet another gentle kiss on my forehead. "Not ever. We were right behind you."

As far as I was concerned, there could have been a marching band following along and still all I would have seen would have been Jared walking toward that glistening blade.

The snowplows dug us out the next day, though as witnesses Jared and I had to stay on to give our statements at least half a dozen times after everyone else left. By the time that ordeal was over, we had discussed things both calmly and emotionally and chosen to give marriage another chance, agreeing that present happiness means more than past pride or future uncertainty.

We were remarried almost immediately. Of course, like most people we have our problems, but now we talk about them and handle them day–by–day. On the whole, I know I'm happier than I've ever been, and I think Jared is too.

Jared is back on the concert circuit; his first symphony booking was less than three months after our wedding. Although he had a slowish start, in another year his name will be bigger than it ever was.

It took me a while, but eventually I started back on *A Man of Honor*. Jared thinks it's going to be a wonderful book, a bigger success than *A Woman of Quality*. Maybe. It was painful at first, but I suppose most good things are. It's almost finished now, and sometimes I find myself thinking how proud Anita would have been of it.

That's not bad praise.

Janis Susan May

About the Author

Like the legendary Auntie Mame, Janis Susan May believes in trying a bit of everything. She has been an advertising executive, a casting director, a banker, a tour guide, an actress, an opera singer, a country music columnist, editor-in-chief of two multi-magazine publishing groups, supervisor of accessioning for a bio-genetic testing laboratory, and photographer. In her younger days, she tried her hand at being a pilot and a race car driver. She has had a nightclub act, done film and television make-up, headed a parapsychological research team, and just finished the narration on an audio book — one she didn't write!

Additionally, Susan recently retired as editor of the Newsletter of the North Texas Chapter of the American Research Center in Egypt, a periodical she founded over twelve years ago that, until recently, was recognized as the only monthly publication for the ARCE in the entire world.

Janis Susan May loves to travel, speaks several languages, and is always up for an adventure. She recently married for the first time, becoming an instant grandmother in the process, and is trying something she has never done before — being a full time housewife.

Look for May's website in the very near future!

Janis Susan May

Vintage Romance Publishing offers the finest in historical romance, inspirational, non-fiction, poetry, and books for children. Visit us on the web at <u>www.vrpublishing.com</u> for more history, more adventure and more titles.

Dark Music

Janis Susan May

Printed in the United States
61622LVS00001B/19-36